DUEL
OF PASSION

Madeleine Ker

Harlequin Books

TORONTO • NEW YORK • LONDON
AMSTERDAM • PARIS • SYDNEY • HAMBURG
STOCKHOLM • ATHENS • TOKYO • MILAN

Original hardcover edition published in 1990
by Mills & Boon Limited

ISBN 0-373-03094-0

Harlequin Romance first edition December 1990

Who was conquering whom, Sophie wondered

"You're so lovely," Kyle whispered raggedly. His hand was caressing her hip, the satiny skin of her thigh. "From the moment I saw you, I've been wanting you. And I know you feel the same way."

"You don't know anything of the kind," she retorted. But she had to speak between his kisses, and the blood was rushing in her veins.

Then she remembered Maisie. Before he could stop her, she slid away from him, rose to her slender shaky legs and ran down the sand to the sea.

The warm water enveloped her, too warm and too salty to do much in the way of rinsing away her emotions—but at least she'd escaped from the drowning maelstrom of Kyle's lovemaking. For the time being....

Madeleine Ker is a self-described "compulsive writer." In fact, Madeleine has been known to deliver six romances in less than a year. She is married and lives in Spain.

Books by Madeleine Ker

CHAPTER ONE

THE rhythm of the Caribbean surf was the most soothing sound Sophie had ever known. It was so different from the pounding of the North Sea, that gravelly hammering she had listened to all her childhood on the North Yorkshire coast; and different, too, from the peaceful lap-lapping of the Mediterranean, the only other sea she'd known.

Lying on her back in the baking sun, her eyes shut behind the opaque sunglasses, she had been listening to the alternate rush and hiss of the ocean waves all morning, wrapped in a world of peace and warmth.

Now and then there had been the distant voices of other people sharing this Jamaican morning; but the exclusive San Antonio Hotel owned the whole white sweep of beach, and since Sophie had walked almost half a mile from the hotel to find the most sheltered spot in it, encircled by rocks and sheltered from the breezes, she'd had the surf and the sun and the sand all to herself all morning.

She hoped it was going to be like this every day for the next three weeks.

For a single girl in her early twenties to have chosen to spend a three-week holiday by herself in Ocho Rios, on the beautiful north coast of Jamaica, was slightly unusual. But then, Sophie Aspen was a slightly unusual person. And she'd had strong reasons for choosing this kind of break.

After less than four days of her holiday, Sophie was already starting to tan a rich golden-brown. Her slim body, as she lay completely relaxed in her black bikini, might have served as a mouth-watering image for some lavish advertisement.

She was tall for a woman, and her figure was delectable, with slender and graceful limbs. The outsize sunglasses covered a lot of her face, but what showed was distinctly interesting: a short, straight nose and a neat chin, framing a full, rather passionate mouth, and an abundance of mahogany-rich hair, now taking on golden highlights under the influence of the sun.

It was the mouth to which one's attention returned. Warm and sexy, it was also determined. There was courage in its curves, evidence that the owner possessed strong and definite feelings. Whatever the eyes were like behind those sunglasses, the casual observer might have guessed that they would be both beautiful and marked by a strong character.

The casual observer, if asked to guess her occupation, might have suggested modelling, the theatre, or television. In fact, all three would have been accurate guesses, because Sophie Aspen had worked intermittently in all three of those fields.

But since leaving drama school she had thought of herself primarily as an actress. That was the goal she had always had throughout her adolescence. During the past two years, however, she had struggled through one of the worst periods for the theatre in recent years, counting herself lucky to have got walk-on parts in minor productions, with the odd bonanza of an appearance in a television commercial. Until last autumn, that was.

Last autumn—in October, to be precise—she had been given her first real, meaty role. And not just in some small company, either; she had landed the part of Maisie Wilkin in *The Elmtree Road Murders*, a glamorous period murder mystery being made by BBC 2's drama department.

The play was scheduled for a peak-viewing two-hour slot this summer, on Thursday the fifteenth of August. Only a few weeks away, in fact.

It had been her biggest break ever, and it had called forth her finest performance so far.

Yet, now, she could not think of *The Elmtree Road Murders* without a touch of sadness. What had started out as such an exciting challenge for her had ended on a note of bitterness and hurt.

It had taken all the eight months since then to get over that hurt.

The past days of swimming and long walks along the beach had already seen a few ounces of excess weight disappear from her hips and thighs, and, in fact, she was slimmer now than she'd ever been since leaving drama school. Her body was honing down to exquisite lines, and her skin was recovering from the awful period of greasy lifelessness it had gone through.

She felt optimistic and healthy...

All that remained to fix now was the old-fashioned hairstyle that she'd worn for the three modern dramas. The hairdressers had advised her to let it grow out before she had it cut.

As soon as she got back to London, she would have to start preparing for her next job: a television commercial for bath oil, scheduled to be filmed in six weeks' time. The fifty-second sequence of her soaping herself languidly in a bathtub would hardly be great theatrical art, but it would certainly pay a few bills!

She would have to contact the art director of the advertising company about her hair. She wanted it cut into something glamorous and short, but she would have to go by what they decided.

There were voices nearby again: the soft laughter of a child, and the husky bass of a man. Too soft to contend with the musical suck and rush of the surf, they scarcely intruded into Sophie's thoughts.

'Give me your hand. Come on, don't be frightened.'

Lazily, Sophie turned her head to half open her eyes. A man, the owner of the bass voice, was hoisting a little girl up to stand on the rocks beside which Sophie was lying. They were against the sun, and through her sunglasses they were just two silhouettes.

'Oh, look at that beautiful boat!'

'Which one?'

'The one with the red sail. There!'

'Ah, yes. That's rather nice. Want one like that for your birthday?'

Something about that husky voice was starting to make Sophie's nerves prickle with tension.

'Uncle Kyle! Look at this.'

Kyle? It couldn't be. Not here! It had to be a figment of her imagination.

Her peaceful reverie had turned into a waking nightmare. She listened tautly as the man answered the child's chattering questions, trying to establish whether that husky voice was the one that had once cut into her with the force of a rhino-hide whip.

The last time she'd heard *that* voice had also been on a beach, almost nine months ago. On that occasion, his words had carried, clear and deep, across the beach. But today the sea and the wind made voices sound different, softer...

'Let's go down there. It looks interesting.'

They were clambering down the rocks towards the little enclave where Sophie lay. Let them not come down here, she prayed hastily. Escape was impossible—there was no way out of her little inlet. But it was too late for prayers. They were down now, and walking towards her.

'Uncle Kyle,' she heard the child exclaim, 'someone's already here!' Then, in a confidential voice, she added, 'Gosh. She's *lovely*.'

Sophie sat up quickly, and lifted her sunglasses to stare at the pair.

'I'm so sorry,' the man said, speaking directly to Sophie. 'We didn't mean to wake you.'

Recognition of that husky voice was superfluous. As soon as she'd looked into the dark-fringed, deep green eyes, she'd felt a giant fist close around her heart and start squeezing.

It was Kyle Hart.

Unbelievably, it *was*. Wearing only a dark blue Speedo that emphasised, rather than concealed, his manifest masculinity, he stood between her and the sea, considering Sophie with that assessing, smouldering gaze she knew so well.

A formidably male face, etched with lines that said he'd lived through plenty of experience, in more departments of life than one. The mouth looked as though it had kissed a thousand women, and had left them all crying for more.

The silvery streaks among the dark, almost black hair said that he was no boy. Yet his potency and vigour were unquestioned. His lithe body was tanned darker than her own, a symphony of lean muscle, emphasised by the dark hair that curled lazily down his flat belly to his loins. His legs were long and muscular, and he had the powerful shoulders and taut waist of a man who took his exercise seriously.

The child beside him was dark-haired and pretty, and was carrying a red plastic bucket full of pebbles and sea shells.

Sophie's throat had been too choked with shock to answer him. She was waiting for him to recognise her, to remember, to say something. She found words with an effort.

'I—I wasn't asleep.'

His gaze was moving down the satiny skin of her body appreciatively, with no sign that he had ever set eyes on her before now. He swung his wide shoulders to glance round her little cove. 'Nice place you have here.' he smiled. '"A fine and private place."'

...But none I think do there embrace. Her memory finished the couplet for her, but her voice was still frozen.

'You *are* English?' he asked, turning the dark green eyes back to her with a quizzical look.

The direct question forced an answer out of her.

'Yes. I'm English.'

He laughed, a pleasant, husky sound. 'For a moment I thought you might be French or Italian. You could be, with that tan, although the grey eyes are a give-away. You're staying at the San Antonio?'

'Yes,' she said again, dry-mouthed.

He considered her blank expression, her hand still holding the sunglasses up against her forehead. 'Are we bothering you?'

'N-not at all.'

He nodded, evidently deciding not to attempt any more conversational gambits, and squatted next to the little girl, hard muscles tightening along his thighs. 'Look at all these lovely shells, Emma. Isn't that a cowrie?'

Together, they wandered away from Sophie, the man holding the child's hand. He didn't look back.

He had stared her straight in the eyes, and hadn't known.

Don't you recognise me? The disbelieving cry was still echoing in Sophie's head as she lowered the sunglasses again, and wrapped her slim arms around her knees.

Her heart was pounding behind her breast-bone, making her breathing quicken involuntarily. What was he doing here?

What perverse fate could have brought him all this way, to land in the very little cove where she had been lying? It just didn't seem possible that his presence here could be a coincidence. Was it possible that there was a connection, that he had followed her here——?

She rejected the idea before it was even half formed, with a flicker of scorn. Of course he hadn't. That was absurd. If he'd wanted to contact her after Brighton, he'd had eight long months to do it in.

And she'd told no one except Joey that she was coming to Jamaica. Hélène didn't know: she was filming in Scotland. No, it had to be coincidence.

Sophie sat in a kind of trance, watching him stroll along the beach with the child, as if the slightest movement would break the spell and make him vanish.

But he didn't vanish. It was Kyle Hart, here in Ocho Rios. She was still getting to grips with the idea. The little girl had called him 'Uncle'. His real niece? The daughter of his current lover? There was no way of telling.

The situation would be almost funny if it weren't so weird. A mad desire to laugh rose up in her. They hadn't seen each other since last October. Had she really changed that much in the eight months since then?

Yes, of course she had changed. Though why should he remember her, whether she'd changed or not? It was as inevitable that he would forget her as that she would remember him with needle-sharp clarity. Their meetings had been brief, forgettable, and he would probably never know how much he had offended her.

A slow, ironic smile tugged at her lips. Well, *he* hadn't changed much, anyway. Kyle Hart was still the most beautiful male animal she had ever set eyes on.

The last time she'd seen him, on Brighton beach at the end of last year, he'd worn an elegant cream linen suit. He was even more magnificent now, more complete, as he wandered semi-naked along a very different beach.

The child laughed happily as she and Kyle moved along the waterline, searching the white sand for treasures. Sophie followed them with grey eyes that were starting to mist behind the sunglasses, as she remembered the way it had all started, in the summer of last year...

'You'll have to put on three stones, of course.'

'What?'

'There's a limit to what padding can achieve. It's the arms and legs, you know. And the face, of course.'

Sophie's agent, Joey Gilmour, had been excited about the role from the very start. He'd felt that it was the right opening for Sophie, and he'd been proved right. Though the big roles had already been earmarked for popular and established actors like Hélène le Bon, there was going to be a sprinkling of new faces in the cast.

And the part of Maisie Wilkin had been one of those scheduled to go to an unknown.

The blackmailing housemaid, Maisie Wilkin, was a grotesque character in every respect. Not only was she a leech who had battened on her erring but beautiful mistress for two years, but she was physically far from inspiring. The scriptwriters had been very firm about that.

Her being plain, overweight and ungainly was an essential part of the story, as Sophie's agent had impressed upon her while he'd been grooming her for the auditions. It explained her bitter jealousy and resentment of her elegant employer's many affairs with men.

Maisie Wilkin was certainly a challenge, a role for a character actress to get her teeth into. If she landed the job of playing Maisie, it would be Sophie's most important part since leaving drama academy. And, considering that a large proportion of that period had been spent sitting in her agent's waiting-room, or casting for parts she'd never got, Sophie had launched into the task of landing Maisie with every ounce of enthusiasm at her disposal.

She had embarked on the task of putting on thirty more pounds of adiposity. Before the audition, Joey had also made her have her hair cut in a hideously unflattering 1920s style, with a parting down the middle, and short, ungainly bangs like spaniel's ears. She'd completed the outfit with low-heeled shoes that reduced her height, old-fashioned horn-rimmed glasses that were alternately like Billy Bunter and a particularly hung-over barn-owl, and a thick coating of sallow make-up.

Similarly, she'd had to overlay her hint of a northern accent with a southern counties intonation. She'd had to unlearn the elegant model's walk that had taken so long to perfect, and had developed a shuffling, flat-footed gait.

It had all been a challenge. But she'd risen to it with the will of one who hadn't worked in a long while, and the results had bowled the casting director over.

'That's it,' she'd all but shouted, as Sophie had finished the speech they'd given her to read. 'That's Maisie Wilkin!'

All she needed, she had been told, was to dye her hair black, and put on just fifteen more pounds.

'It'll come off again in a flash,' she'd been assured, 'and it really is essential for the part. Don't you like cream cakes?'

'Well, yes——'

'Just let yourself go, darling. Fifteen pounds'll go on in no time. Frankly, an order like that is my idea of heaven!'

That was the way it had begun.

The first time she had met Kyle Hart had been several weeks after that.

It had been in Brighton, during the final stages of filming *The Elmtree Road Murders*, before they'd gone back to London to do the courtroom scenes. She remembered it all so well. It had been at a stage when she'd been most preoccupied with her characterisation, and most concerned to give a good performance in her first major role.

She and Hélène had eaten in the mobile canteen, in the courtyard of the rambling old boarding-house where they'd been filming. the two of them had been alone at a table, under an umbrella to shade them from the morning sun.

Hélène had had the chicken salad, and Sophie had had a pie and chips. She'd been asking Hélène for some precious advice about her role, and Hélène had said something about Maisie being a crow...

'Of course it's a challenge for you, darling,' Hélène had said. 'Maisie Wilkin is a crow, and you're a swan.'

'I don't feel very swanlike at this moment.'

'You're not *meant* to, darling. You're meant to be a very plain, overweight, dim-witted, nasty-minded housemaid. It's a part I would have given my eye-teeth for at your age.'

Sophie smiled. Slim, elegant, and looking ravishing in the 1920s suit she'd worn for that morning's filming, Hélène le Bon was luminously beautiful as she studied the menu.

The mobile canteen wasn't renowed for its cuisine, which was why some of the cast chose to eat in restaurants in Brighton. Sophie and Hélène, however, always ate in the canteen—Hélène because she was utterly indifferent to food, and Sophie because she was too shy about her appearance to venture far from the set these days.

Like Hélène, she was still in costume. If you could call a shabby pinafore, wrinkled stockings and a lumpy grey cardigan a costume.

Unlike Hélène, she hadn't been dressed that way by choice. The trouble with having put on thirty pounds was that almost nothing of her own fitted her any more, which meant that she was forced to wear Maisie Wilkin's clothes around the set.

She certainly wasn't going to equip herself with a whole new size eighteen wardrobe just for the duration of *The Elmtree Road Murders*, because the first thing she was going to do once the last foot of film was in the can was go on a crash diet.

A diet which didn't include a single ounce of any fat, oil or carbohydrate.

'I'm going to have the chicken salad,' Hélène decided. She glanced at Sophie with a glint of amusement. 'You'd better have the pie and chips, Maisie. Don't want you losing your figure.'

'Do I have to?'

'You're starting to melt away, unless I'm much mistaken.'

Sophie wriggled in her grimy beige pinafore. It was certainly looser on her these days. If she lost any more weight, Percy Schumaker, the director, would start complaining again.

'You're right. I definitely have trouble identifying with Maisie's diet,' she smiled, sitting back in the chair.

'What exactly is worrying you about your performance?'

'I don't really know, Hélène.' She fidgeted with her ring. Even that was tight, these days. 'I just feel I'm not getting to the depths of my part. Maybe I'm simply not experienced enough an actress to cope with a role like Maisie.'

'Oh, nonsense. You're doing a marvellous job, darling. But if you feel you're not getting deep enough down into Maisie, perhaps the answer is that you're not . . .' Hélène le Bon frowned as she searched for the word, her slim eyebrows drawing down in a V over luminous brown eyes. '. . . perhaps not *compassionate* enough towards her.'

The waitress brought their food, and Sophie contemplated her pie, which was swimming in gravy and surrounded by glistening chips, with distaste. Feeling eyes on her, she'd looked up, and met the gaze of a handsome blond man a few tables away. He was one of the extras, and she'd noticed him several times. He had the kind of rugged looks that appealed to her, and a fine, athletic figure.

But as her eyes met his he looked away hastily, and started talking animatedly to the woman next to him.

Sophie, flushing, tackled her pie and chips with the true Maisie Wilkin spirit of grim doggedness.

Men never used to look away from her. In fact, the looks she used to get were downright appreciative. And now . . .

She brought her mind back to acting. 'Not compassionate enough?' she echoed.

'Yes,' Hélène nodded. 'I don't mean pity. That's something else. I mean understanding. During the scenes we're shooting here, it isn't that important. But once we're back in London you'll certainly have to dig a little deeper into Maisie.'

Within a fortnight they were due to conclude the location filming here in Brighton, and take the circus back to London. The climax of *The Elmtree Road Murders*, the trial and the emotional courtroom scenes, would be done in the studios after the boarding-house scenes were over.

'The trial is the real heart of the film, you see. It's where we get to see what Patricia and Maisie are really like inside, and the deep-down reasons why they acted as they did. The focus is very much on character and motive. This is your time to shine, Sophie. Those final speeches of yours—well, I think you can see how effective they could be if you treated them right.'

Sophie concentrated. Advice from Hélène le Bon was worth rubies. 'How do you mean, treated them right?'

'Well, up until now your part has been all motiveless malignity,' Hélène had said. 'After all, Maisie has been really rather vicious. Blackmail, betrayal, hypocrisy. The audience isn't exactly captivated with her morals.' She leaned forward. 'But in those courtroom speeches, you can give a real *cri de coeur*. You can make the audience feel what it's really like to be someone like Maisie Wilkin—ugly, slighted, disadvantaged, the kind of person nobody really bothers to understand until it's too late. You can leave them with a feeling of compassion, almost of wonder...'

Hélène was, by her own admission, pushing forty-five. A deeply experienced and much-loved actress, she could have been a very intimidating person for Sophie, twenty-three and in her first significant role, to play against. But Hélène had taken her under her wing from the start, and Percy Schumaker was a good enough director to let Hélène guide Sophie through the part without contradicting her judgements too much.

Sophie listened in attentive silence as Hélène outlined the emotional peaks and valleys of the scenes that lay ahead. Though she knew the script backwards, it always astounded Sophie how much light Hélène could shed on characters other than the one she herself was playing. She had the true actress's ability to empathise with all the roles in a script, and she made Sophie feel hopelessly amateurish at times.

She'd been listening so intently to Hélène that she hadn't noticed the tall figure that had approached their table, and was now looming over them.

That was when Kyle Hart had first appeared in her life.

Despite the Caribbean warmth, a shiver of goose-flesh now swept across Sophie's tanned skin as the memory flooded back.

Her eyes, which had lost their focus while she'd thought back, now flicked to the tall figure of Kyle Hart, stooping twenty yards away from her with the child.

That moment would stay with her for a long time. The recognition that she was looking into the eyes of one of the most beautiful men she would ever meet.

Not that she'd been conscious of the rest of his face at first. It had been Kyle's eyes that had electrified her.

Though he hadn't been as dark in Brighton as he was now, his skin had been tanned enough to make those tawny-green eyes as cool and startling as lake-water in some sandstone desert. They had held a directness that was animal, shocking. Utterly sure of his own strength.

For a split second, Sophie had met that heart-stopping gaze with unthinking, wide-eyed shock. Then she'd remembered what she looked like, and how he must see her, and embarrassment had washed over her in a tide that had flushed her plump cheeks crimson.

'Kyle!' Hélène had risen to give him a hug and a kiss, then had introduced him to Sophie as Kyle Hart, a financier in the City, and one of her oldest friends.

The fact that he was smiling at them both had softened the lines of what she'd instinctively known would be a merciless face in repose, darkly virile. His self-assurance went with not having to question his own sexuality, mastery or wealth.

Sophie had felt a keen sense of frustration. If only this magnificent male had chosen to arrive in her life a few weeks earlier, he would have met a reasonably pretty woman, reasonably poised, and reasonably attractive.

As it was, those green eyes had glittered with inner amusement at a frightful, overweight frump with greasy black hair and owlish glasses, wearing the most unflattering garments ever devised by a satanic wardrobe-mistress, and quailing into her seat with embarrassment and shame.

Not that Kyle Hart had betrayed his contempt in any way then, or during the days that had followed.

Kyle's relationship with Hélène was warm and intimate; though she was older than he was, they were evidently good friends, sharing a lot in common. He had been in Brighton on business to do with the merchant bank for which he worked, and had dropped into the set regularly, watching the filming from the sidelines. Obviously a connoisseur of acting, he had complimented them both on their performances.

He'd also been very kind in other ways. He'd taken them both out, twice to lunch, three times to dinner, invariably at the best restaurants in town.

Sophie had done the best she possibly could to eradicate Maisie on those occasions, but no amount of make-up could have hidden the extra pounds, the lank black hair, and the awful clothes she'd been forced to wear. Even the heavy black glasses had had to go with her: she needed them for reading, and she'd got into the habit of twitching them on and off nervously.

In any case, they had been finishing off the Brighton episodes, and there was no way she could have got too far out of Maisie's character and still kept the integrity of her performance in front of the cameras.

And, despite all that, she'd let herself nurture those crazy delusions. Delusions that it was herself, and not Hélène, that Kyle was really interested in. That it was by his wish that she went everywhere with them, rather than through Hélène's kindness. That he could look under the surface of her less-than-beautiful image, and see the woman beneath.

Not exactly experienced with men, she had found her contact with this devastatingly handsome, sophisticated, witty tiger dazzling. He had had an impact on her emotions that had bowled her over.

What was so exciting was that it went beyond a physical attraction. They shared so much in common, it seemed. They both loved the theatre, the same kind of music, had the same views about so many things. Kyle was amused by the same odd moments that made her laugh, and they shared an off-beat sense of humour, so that they two had sometimes been helpless with laughter at things that had made Hélène only smile in puzzlement.

Kyle, in fact, had been flatteringly attentive towards Sophie, and so apparently interested in her, her views and her work that her stupid head had been utterly turned.

Oh, the fluttering heart, the shallow breathing, the hot, mad dreams!

Sophie's fingers clenched into tight fists, her nails digging into her palms as if to punish herself for her incredible stupidity. Had she really imagined that a man like Kyle could have been seriously interested in someone like Maisie Wilkin?

Yes, she had. She forced herself to conjure up the misery all over again.

She'd fallen into an infatuation swifter and deeper than anything she'd known before. Dreaming of the day when she could cast off Maisie, and present herself to Kyle as she really was, she had been drawn into something she'd never had as a schoolgirl—a schoolgirl crush. And the fact that her emotions had been as yet largely untried had made the crush all the more fierce, all the more hopeless.

She'd been like a convert exposed to a new religion, embracing her passion without thought or logic. Like a teenager in the front row of a matinée, dreaming an impossible dream.

Until the memorable afternoon of her disillusionment.

Then, as now, they had been on the beach. Taking a break during the late afternoon filming, she and Hélène and Kyle had walked from the set down to the beach with a party of the crew and the cast.

It had been a mild, warm autumn day, with no hint of the winter that was to come. Hélène and Kyle had gone off for a walk on their own. After twenty minutes, Sophie had followed, hands thrust into the pockets of her housecoat as she trudged barefoot across the warm pebbly beach, her thoughts happy and free.

She'd come upon them sitting on a pair of deck-chairs, facing the sea.

The stiff breeze had been flowing inland, from them towards Sophie. Which was how they hadn't heard her approach.

And why she'd caught every word of their conversation.

'Oh, come on, Hélène,' Kyle had been saying, his voice somewhere between frustration and amusement. 'Why don't you speak to the girl about her appearance? She's like an overweight owl!'

Sophie had frozen where she'd stood, the blood draining away from her heart.

'Sophie isn't that overweight,' Hélène had rebuked.

'Well, she's not exactly sylph-like.'

'She's a splendid young actress, and she's doing an excellent job with a difficult role.'

'Maybe so, but her appearance is absurd. She wears such terrible clothes, not to mention her hair—how could any young girl let herself go like that? She must have no pride in herself whatsoever.'

'You don't understand, Kyle.' Hélène's voice had been patient. 'Sophie isn't normally like that. She hasn't "let herself go", as you so crudely put it. She's supposed to be unattractive, for the part. You'll understand why when you see the film.'

'Well, if she's supposed to be unattractive, she certainly fits the bill.'

'Is she getting on your nerves?'

'She does rather irritate me, snatching those glasses off and on like a railway signal the whole time.'

'Well, she's embarrassed about them.' Hélène had lit a cigarette, and Sophie had numbly watched the smoke drifting towards her. 'Sophie's had to put on nearly three stones to play Maisie,' she had explained. 'So, naturally, her own wardrobe doesn't fit her any more. She has to wear Maisie's clothes. The hair's dyed, of course. And she's even gone to the length of having her own lenses fitted into those heavy black frames. That's why she looks like an owl to you. You're really looking at someone in heavy disguise. If you can't see that underneath it all she's a very intelligent, pretty girl——'

'I'll grant you the intelligence. She's good company, poor thing. But *pretty*?'

'Yes. She has a beautiful face.'

'If you think suet pudding is beautiful.' Kyle's laughter had been soft, mocking.

'You're cruel,' Hélène had said. 'I've rather taken her under my wing, you see.'

'Yes, I've noticed. Another of your lame ducks. She doesn't benefit from the comparison, I assure you. Do you know what she looks like, next to you?'

'Kyle, don't. Sophie Aspen is very far from being a lame duck. She's just young, and rather inexperienced. It's good for her to be around a sophisticated man like you. That's why I like to have her along with us. And you've been very sweet to her so far. Think of it as a charity.'

'Yes, well, I've been a little too charitable, I think.'

'Hmm?'

'You can't mean you haven't noticed?' Kyle had demanded, the husky laugh drifting back to where Sophie had stood like stone on the twilight beach. 'The poor girl is falling in love with me.'

'Oh, dear,' Hélène had sighed. 'I think you're right. I have noticed her being rather moony in your presence.'

'There's no doubt about it. I know the signs. It would be amusing if it weren't so pathetic.'

'Well, you're used to that, at least,' Hélène had smiled. 'And I can assure you that you've had less worthy women than Sophie Aspen in love with you.'

'Have I? I've certainly had slimmer.'

'I just hope that you're not going to——'

'Laugh in her face?' Kyle had concluded for her. 'No, Hélène, I'll restrain myself from that. Though it won't be easy. She looks like . . .'

Kyle had gone on to describe exactly what she'd looked like. He had a talent with words. He could make them glitter like surgeons' knives, could make them stab and slash and puncture the flimsy bubble of vanity and illusion.

But Sophie hadn't stayed to hear the end of it.

She'd willed her paralysed legs to start moving, to turn around and carry her bleeding soul back towards the others, where she'd come from.

There wasn't any way she could describe how she'd been feeling. The pain and humiliation had been glowing in her, like coals in a stove. It had been something she'd known she would never forget.

To see ourselves as others saw us—a gift that could be terrible. But he hadn't needed to be so cruel! The frivolous, superficial, callous pig——

If she could have confronted him there and then, and thrown it all back in his face, she would have done. But the awful thing was that everything he'd said about her had been true.

She *had* been infatuated with him. And she *had* been an absurd sight. It was just that she'd forgotten. And had forgotten how much value the world placed on images. She'd known that she'd looked less than ravishing, but she hadn't known just how important appearances were to people.

Kyle hadn't known her at all. That was what had really hurt her. He'd never looked beneath the surface. He'd never bothered to see beneath the exterior, to the real person she was under the dyed hair and thick make-up, the ugly glasses, the extra weight, the shabby clothes.

He'd never bothered to find out that she wasn't absurd inside, that she wasn't some kind of freak. To him, she'd never been Sophie Aspen at all. She'd only been Maisie, a physically unattractive woman whose so-obvious infatuation with him had been laughable, a thing to hold in contempt...

Well, pain was valuable to an actress. It was like raw stone to a sculptor. And this pain was Kyle Hart's own special contribution to her development as an actress. He had changed her, had shown her a great deal about the world, and the way the world was obsessed with appearances. And for that, she felt a kind of bitter gratitude.

But, for the rest, he was a man she would loathe for the rest of her life.

That night she'd excused herself from the dinner that Kyle had offered, pleading an upset tummy. He had been exceptionally kind to her that night, and over the next few days until he had left Brighton to go back to the City. Kind! That had been the final straw. His scorn she could live with. His kindness could go to the devil! She had not gone out with him again, despite pressing invitations. And she'd never spoken to him again.

Not until ten minutes ago, at least.

Though her hurt and anger had lain too deep for words, it had been within her powers to act out her feelings on the set.

And the understanding of her role that had eluded her until then had suddenly been there, shimmering in her performance the next morning.

During the last days at Brighton, and the final episodes in the studio, she'd brought a quality of fury against the world to Maisie Wilkin that had made Percy Schumaker kiss her on both cheeks, and the studio crew give her standing ovations on several occasions.

It was as if, for the first time, she had really known what it was like to be someone like Maisie Wilkin—ugly, slighted, disadvantaged, the kind of person nobody really bothered to understand until it was too late.

Sophie had never spoken to Hélène about what she'd heard that afternoon on the beach.

Once or twice, she'd caught Hélène staring at her as though she'd half suspected the truth, but neither of them had ever brought it up. Nor had Sophie ever laid the slightest blame at Hélène's door. To her, Hélène le Bon would always be someone who had helped her profoundly in her career, and since *The Elmtree Road Murders* they had remained friends.

'You're a very talented actress,' Hélène had said gently, on the last day of filming. 'You have a bright future ahead of you, Sophie.'

But she'd been drained and exhausted by the time filming had ended.

Her first concern, once filming had ended last November, had been to slough off Maisie Wilkin, the way a snake shed its unwanted skin. She had gone back to her St John's Wood flat, and had retreated deep into her shell, had embarked on a crash diet, had seen no one, gone nowhere. She had superintended the eradication of Maisie without sorrow or remorse. Diet and exercise had taken care of the extra weight. The black hair-dye had washed out, and the rest had been mainly cosmetic.

Getting back to work, she had spent the first five months of this year touring with a repertory company, staging a trio of very modern dramas called *Here*, *There*, and *Nowhere*, which had never played to more than half-full houses. It had been her second substantial job in acting, but it had been far from a success. Most of the cast had been young hopefuls, like herself. She, in fact, with her experience of television, had been better off than most of them.

The pay had been minimal, the conditions had been exhausting, and everyone had let out a silent sigh of relief when the director had finally announced, at the beginning of June, that the tour was folding. None of them had been paid for more than three months out of the five. Without her fee from *The Elmtree Road Murders*, which she'd been hoarding in her building-society account, she would have had a thin time of it.

When the tour had folded, Sophie had found herself at a loose end. And she'd been very run down. After the pain of what had happened in Brighton, the débâcle of *Here*, *There*, and *Nowhere* had taken a lot out of her. She'd felt that she desperately needed a break, some kind of sun-drenched holiday to restore her calm and help bring back her dented self-respect.

She'd seen the cancellation in the travel agent's window. Though the price of the holiday had been halved, it was still expensive. And three weeks was longer than she'd wanted to go for. But she'd felt somehow drawn to the idea, and the lure of Jamaica had been irresistible in the end. She'd dipped into her little hoard from *The Elmtree Road Murders*, and had bought the ticket, hoping she was doing the right thing.

She was now feeling that three weeks of sun, sea, and salads were definitely going to be the right thing. She hadn't needed to come all this way just to get a tan and relax. But she'd needed the psychological break, and the

glamour of Jamaica was proving marvellously ben-
eficial to her weary psyche, as it was to her physical well-
being.

She'd tried so hard to forget Kyle over the disastrous
five months of the tour. But, at the end of it all, she
knew she had only half conquered the hurt. It was still
there, inside her, overlaid with a veil that any casual word
could whisk away.

That was really why she had come to Jamaica. Because of Kyle Hart. To get over him once and for all.

And now he was walking towards her, on a sun-
drenched beach in Ocho Rios, and he didn't even know
who she was.

CHAPTER TWO

IT WAS the child who reached her first.

'I've found some beautiful shells,' she said, sitting down next to Sophie and overturning her bucket of treasures to sort through them. 'Aren't they lovely?'

'Lovely.'

''Course, most of them are broken,' the child sighed. 'You have to go diving to get the ones that aren't broken. My uncle's going to dive for me soon. Look—mother o'pearl!'

'That's very pretty,' Sophie said, taking the shell from the child. Her pulse-rate was just settling down to normal as Kyle approached.

He looked down at her speculatively. 'This is going to sound rather weak—but we've met somewhere before, haven't we?'

'No.' The lie came to her mouth at once, unbidden. 'No, I don't think we have.'

'Well, then you remind me very strongly of someone I've met once before, though I can't think who.' Suddenly he smiled. 'That sounds like the crudest kind of come-on line, doesn't it? Worse than "do you come here often?"'

Sophie smiled blankly. She didn't want him to recognise her, not any more.

Kyle was taller than she had remembered, a big, leanly built man who wore his rangy body with the assurance of complete authority. In Brighton, the naked power of his body had been cloaked in linen and silk. Out here, practically naked but for the black triangle of his swimming-trunks, he made Sophie aware of the aggressive mastery that burned in his every movement. It was as though she could physically see the calm, potent

27

maturity that set Kyle apart from every man she'd ever met before.

'Can I ask you your name?'

'Sophie Webb.' Again, she hadn't meant to lie. The words had just been there in her mouth. Actually, it was almost the truth—Sophie Webb Aspen was her full name. Would 'Sophie' ring any bells?

Apparently not.

'My name's Kyle Hart. And this is Emma, my niece.'

'Pleased to meet you,' Emma smiled, and wandered off down to the water's edge to look for more shells.

Kyle sat down in the space his niece had vacated, the warm skin of his shoulder brushing hers for a moment, making her flinch as though she'd been touched with a hot branding-iron. 'We're also staying in the San Antonio. We arrived yesterday.'

'Are you with Emma's parents?'

'No.' He glanced at the figure of the little girl. 'My brother and his wife are going through a rough patch with their marriage. In fact, they're on the brink of a separation. I volunteered to take Emma on holiday, partly to get her away from the atmosphere at home, and partly to give her parents a breathing-space. A chance to save their marriage before the ultimate break-up.'

'I see.'

That was why he was here. At least she now knew who Emma was, and why Kyle was in Jamaica. Her idea that he'd come to find her had been just as absurd as she'd known it would be.

'And you?' He glanced at her briefly. 'Are you here with friends?'

'I'm on my own,' she replied.

He didn't look surprised, but she sensed that he was. 'Your first visit to Jamaica?'

'Yes.'

'England to the Caribbean is a long way to come on your own.' His expression told her he was still puzzled by her, still trying to place her. 'May I ask what you do for a living?'

'I'm ... a model.'

'That figures,' he smiled, his eyes drifting over her figure. 'I'm afraid my own occupation is nothing so glamorous. I work in a bank.'

'Really?' The tension was too much for her. Making small talk with Kyle was just too much. She knew that if she didn't get away now she would say or do something really stupid.

With nervous movements, Sophie gathered up her towel and straw bag, and rose fluidly to her feet. 'I'm awfully sorry,' she said, 'but it's time for me to get out of the sun.'

He glanced up at her, dark lashes veiling a slow smile. His eyes took in the honey-tanned length of her body, slow and sultry as a caress, before he spoke. 'You should have said at once if my presence disturbed you.'

'No,' she replied, slightly breathless, 'I really am too hot. I'm going to have a shower before lunch.'

'Then I might see you at lunch?' He couldn't see her eyes behind the dark glasses, but his glance was disturbingly penetrating all the same.

'Of course,' Sophie replied, turning away. 'You might.'

She walked quickly up the beach away from him. She felt his eyes dwelling on her back, and knew in her bones that he was watching the swing of her long legs.

By the time she got back to the hotel her skin was damp with nerves. She took the lift up to her room, wriggled out of her bikini, and stepped under a cool shower.

Whew! What a weirdly tense little experience that had been!

Well, if nothing else, that chance meeting with Kyle Hart had just boosted her ego by several degrees. She'd come here to unwind, to relax, and to restore her self-image. If he didn't even recognise her any more, then her self-image was well and truly restored!

She evidently presented a very different picture from the one she'd presented last autumn.

She felt a smile creep across her lips. What had possessed her to tell him she was a model called Sophie Webb? Mischievously, she was now pleased she had done so. Let him find out who she really was, if he could. She was going to enjoy seeing the look on his face when he did!

She stepped out of the shower, brown and dripping, and dried herself.

Saying that he worked in a bank was almost more of an untruth than her own claim to be a model. She knew that he was, in fact, a partner in a very prestigious firm of merchant bankers, and that 'Hart' was one of the names carved over the lintel of the neo-classical building in the City.

But what she'd said was also at least partly true. She'd done a fair bit of modelling for fashion magazines, especially during her time at drama school, and if her acting career didn't work out she might be doing a lot more in the future. She had never commanded anything like good pay, of course, but it had helped to pay the rent and tuition fees.

So she hadn't really lied to him.

There was, in fact, no immediate prospect of further work for Sophie. Joey Gilmour, her American-born agent, had assured her that in the wake of *The Elmtree Road Murders* there would be further offers, which was always a possibility. She was hoping that her substantial fee from the film, plus what she made from the bath-oil ad, would tide her over until something else came in.

In any case, she wasn't here to worry.

Sophie dressed in a light and airy blue and green dress that brought out the naturally rich colouring of her hair and skin. She looped a string of rose-quartz beads round her neck. The jewellery wasn't expensive, but against her throat the colours glowed prettily.

Come to think of it, this situation might be fun, after all. And perhaps, for once, she would have a more interesting companion over lunch than the thick paperback she was still only a third of the way through.

Would he join her at her table? Would he have remembered who she was since this morning?

She touched her lips with a pink lip-gloss, and went down to lunch feeling as though she were going on stage.

He hadn't recalled her yet. He and Emma joined her table, and all ordered the same thing: a light salad with cold meats. Sophie was now feeling a lot more poised in his company, and was drily awaiting the moment when it suddenly dawned on him who she was.

'Do you always wear those sunglasses?' Kyle enquired, leaning back in his chair to survey her.

'My eyes aren't used to this bright sunlight.' Actually, the sunglasses had prescription lenses, and she could see much more clearly with them. Not that he would know that—the Dior frames looked anything but practical.

'Or is it that you don't want to be recognised?' he asked lazily. Sophie couldn't stop herself from jumping, but he went on, 'After all, you must be a fairly famous model.'

'Why should I be so famous?'

'This place doesn't come cheap,' he shrugged, glancing round the glamorous palm-lined dining-room. 'Money means success. And, in your line of work, success means fame.'

She ate a mouthful of salad before answering. 'I'm not famous, and I probably never will be. I certainly don't want to be.'

'That's a very unfeminine sentiment.' The wicked smile made him suddenly dazzlingly handsome. It was the smile and the eyebrows that gave his face such a cruel cast, she realised suddenly. The dark brows curved down over those tawny eyes in a way that conveyed passion, and the level grin, inlaid with beautiful white teeth, held a predatory quality, the smile on the face of a tiger. 'I assume that's why you look so familiar,' he said, pouring the fresh orange juice that the waiter had brought. 'You must have been on the cover of a magazine at some time, and I'll have seen your face on the news-stands. Something like *Vogue*, I'd guess.'

Sophie shook her head, trying not to laugh. 'Not *Vogue*. But you've probably seen my face here and there.'

'Where would I have been likely to see it?'

'Here and there,' she repeated, shrugging her slender shoulders.

Kyle smiled again at her evasive reply. 'Mystery lady,' he said softly. 'You don't like answering questions, do you?'

'I just don't like talking about myself.'

'Another unfeminine quality,' he observed. Sophie watched his hands as he cut his food. Strong, capable hands, the knuckles etched with glinting hair. On his wrist he wore a black diver's watch, evidently expensive, but not flashy. She knew he was a wealthy man, but he adopted few of the accoutrements of wealth. He didn't adorn himself with gold jewellery or conspicuous clothes, as if he didn't need to prove anything.

'As for the cost of this holiday,' she said, sipping the orange juice, 'I assure you it's an unwonted extravagance, and not the sort of thing I do every six months.'

'You must be rewarding yourself for something, then.'

'Exactly,' Sophie said. He couldn't see the glint in her grey eyes behind the sunglasses, but he caught the tone in her voice.

'Intriguing,' he purred. 'May I ask what?'

'Oh . . . having come through something.'

'What?'

'Something private.'

He grimaced. 'And the curtain comes down again, leaving the mystery intact.'

She put down her knife and fork, and propped her neat chin on her clasped hands. 'I just felt I needed a break from work. I finished a tough assignment a while ago, and I was a bit run down, so I decided to get away from it all. There's nothing mysterious about that at all.'

'It's a mystery to me that you should have decided to come to a place like Jamaica all on your own,' Kyle replied calmly, finishing his grapefruit, and breaking a roll. 'A woman with your beauty and personality shouldn't have to endure solitude.'

The irony of it all kept laughter bubbling just beneath the surface of her deliberately cool poise. The man who'd once described her as an overweight owl with a face like suet pudding, among other things, was sitting here complimenting her on her beauty and charm. Such was the power of a slight change in appearance.

'To me, solitude is a gift, rather than a penance,' she told him. She was rather enjoying her Mystery Lady role. She could see that it piqued and intrigued him, and there was no harm in hamming it up a little. 'I like to get away from the madding crowd from time to time.'

'Can I go and play now?' Emma demanded, plainly bored with the adult conversation.

'Go on,' Kyle nodded. 'But stay out of the sun, or you'll roast.' He watched the little girl scamper off, then turned to her with a smile. 'This is the first time she's been abroad. She's a real London child. Do you live in London?'

'Yes, nowadays. But I grew up in Scarborough.'

'Where the Fair is? Parsley, sage, rosemary and thyme?'

'The same,' she smiled.

He considered her thoughtfully. 'Well, well. A country girl. I wouldn't have thought it. You have the poise of someone whose ancestors danced the gavotte.'

'My ancestors were Yorkshire farming folk. My father has a small sheep-farm—just twenty acres of moorland, really, overlooking the sea.'

'Is it pretty?'

'I think it's lovely.'

He studied the elegant, sophisticated woman in front of him. 'And may I ask how you got the Yorkshire out of your voice?'

'It's still there, if you listen. Or would you rather I prefaced every sentence with ee ba gum?'

He grinned. 'Any more at home like you?'

'I haven't any brothers or sisters, if that's what you mean.'

'Ah. So that explains why you're always so collected. You never had any competition as a child.'

'Oh, I wouldn't say that,' Sophie said wryly. 'My cousin Jenny gave me as much competition as half a dozen sisters!'

'She sounds like quite a girl,' Kyle smiled.

'She's two years younger than me, but she's a real beauty. Much prettier than I'll ever be.'

'Really?' he said, his disbelief flattering.

'She's the one who ought to be the model, but she's got more brains as well as more looks. She's studying maths at the University of York now.'

'What a paragon she must be,' Kyle said gently.

'If I were the jealous type,' she assured him, 'I could get quite worked up about Jenny.'

He studied her. 'Has she the same rich chestnut hair and cool grey eyes?'

'Oh, she puts me in the shade. She has the most beautiful hair, long and golden-red, and bright blue eyes. We grew up together. Her mother and mine are very close. As a child, I was always being asked why I wasn't more like my cousin Jennifer.' Sophie couldn't help her lips tightening slightly. 'When we got older, she used to steal all my boyfriends.'

His eyes were warm. 'But not any more?'

'Well, she meets enough men of her own at university nowadays. But it's a good job I've moved to London. I never particularly like losing my favourite men to my younger cousin.'

Kyle looked amused. But it was the truth. She knew for a fact that Jenny was sexually far more experienced than she herself was. They had always been a paradoxical pair—Jenny, the scientist, supposed to be so cool and precise, yet in her teens an expert on men; Sophie, the actress, who had still, at twenty-three, never been made love to by a man . . .

She had finished eating. And he still didn't know who she was. 'Well,' she said lightly, rising, 'please excuse me. I'm going to have a little lie-down until it's cool enough to swim.'

He rose with automatic courtesy. 'See you on the beach, then,' he said.

She felt his eyes boring into her back as she walked away.

'There's something very familiar about you, Sophie Webb.'

Sophie's poise didn't falter in the slightest as she looked up from the breakfast table a few mornings later.

He'd said that twice over the past few days. Whenever they had met, in fact. But if he hadn't recognised her by now, after all the hours he'd spent in her company, he wasn't going to recognise her this morning, with her wearing her sunglasses and a wide-brimmed straw hat as she breakfasted on the hotel terrace, against a backdrop of palms and blue sea.

She was wearing a pale gold sun-dress over her metallic scarlet one-piece costume, and the colour made her toffee-tanned skin look lusciously smooth.

'It's a little late for that line, isn't it?' she said with light irony. 'Maybe you should ask me if I come here often.'

'I'm being serious,' he smiled, standing in front of her. 'As I came on to the terrace, it struck me again. You're very like somebody I've met once before, but I just can't place who or when. Can I join you for breakfast?'

'If you insist on sharing your every meal with me,' she said gently, 'people are going to talk.'

They'd got into the habit of lunching together, and had had dinner together the night before, too. He sat down anyway, looking amused. 'I'll take the chance on my reputation. And, considering that we're both here on our own...'

She scooped the seeds out of her papaw, and gave him a glance. He was wearing trousers and a loose cotton shirt, open to show the tanned column of his throat. He looked stunning. She forced herself to keep up the light, cool tone she'd adopted from their very first exchanges. 'Considering we're both here on our own?' she prompted.

'Well, eating at the same table is hardly cohabitation.' He picked up the menu. 'Sleep well last night?'

'Fine,' she lied. 'Where's Emma?'

'Coming in a minute. I'm starting to realise that I'm not very good at dealing with grooming an eight-year-old girl.' He turned to the waiter who had materialised beside them, and ordered grapefruit, rolls and coffee. Sophie took advantage of the waiter's presence to ask for a fresh pot of Earl Grey tea.

They'd spent most of yesterday afternoon on the beach, talking and swimming, and he hadn't suspected for a moment that he knew her.

Last night, over their dinner of lobster, oysters and a variety of seafoods, she'd wondered if memory would return. After all, it wasn't exactly the first time that Kyle Hart had faced her across a restaurant table.

But though he'd frowned, and kept probing her for information about herself, recognition had not dawned. Nor, on the other hand, had he made any secret of his attraction towards the woman he still thought of as a stranger met by chance on holiday. He'd made no effort to hide the fact that he was interested in her. Very interested.

She'd looked into those tawny-green eyes last night, and had seen the speculation in them. She knew he was intrigued by her. And she'd remembered that this man had once had to restrain himself from laughing in her face.

Well, now the boot was on the other foot. Now it was she who had to bite back her amusement, to stop herself from telling him what a complete fool he was making of himself.

Would he ever see Sophie Aspen as she really was?

History was repeating itself. Once again, Kyle Hart's eyes hadn't looked beneath the surface. Once again, he was focusing on the external image. Once again, her appearance was all that mattered to him, as though what she was inside was irrelevant. The only difference was that last time he had seen only Maisie Wilkin, the overweight owl. This time he was seeing only Sophie Webb, mysterious and attractive model.

It had been on the tip of her tongue several times over the past few days to tell him who she was, and see the look on his face as realisation set in. But, as it had grown clearer that he still didn't have the remotest idea who she was, she'd decided not to tell him. Not yet, anyway. She was waiting to see how things would turn out.

And things were turning out in a rather amusing way.

He had even kissed her goodnight after dinner last night. She'd just let his lips touch her cheek before she'd drawn quickly away, and with a faint smile had locked herself into her room.

Once, she'd have given her right arm for a kiss from Kyle Hart.

Now, knowing what she did about his shallowness, his cruelty, his superficiality, she was left cold by him.

Almost.

Emma arrived to join them. The eight-year-old had taken a strong fancy to Sophie over the past few days, and she was chattering brightly as she clambered up on to the chair next to her.

'Are you coming to the beach this morning?' she asked hopefully.

'Yep.' Sophie pulled down the shoulder of her sun-dress to show the red strap of her costume against her brown skin. 'I'm all ready.'

'Great! Can we come?'

'I'll think about it,' Sophie smiled. 'What do you fancy for breakfast?'

'Kippers and scrambled egg,' came the unhesitating reply. 'It's my favourite.'

'No kippers,' Sophie said regretfully, consulting the menu.

'Kingfish and ackee come pretty close,' Kyle suggested. 'Kingfish isn't kippers, and ackee isn't egg, but I think you'll enjoy it.'

'OK,' the child conceded. 'I'm going to build a huge sand-castle this morning, bigger than yesterday.'

'Her father,' Kyle smiled, 'is an architect.'

'What *is* ackee?' Sophie wanted to know, after they'd given the order to the waiter. 'I've seen it on the menu every morning, but I've never risked it.'

Kyle was trying to put Emma's dark curls into order. Competent as his long fingers were, they weren't doing much of a job. 'It's very tasty,' he said. 'Actually, it's a fruit, but it ends up a vegetable equivalent of scrambled egg. It was introduced by Captain Bligh.'

'The *Mutiny on the Bounty* man?'

'Yes,' he nodded. 'Another odd thing about it—it's poisonous until it's ripe, and then it sort of pops open, ready to cook.'

'Here.' She took pity on his amateurish efforts with Emma's hair. 'Let me do that. What do you want, Emma, a plait or pigtails?'

'Pigtails,' Emma decided. Sophie found rubber bands and a comb in her beachbag, and started neatening the child's hair, watched by Kyle. 'How do you know so much about Jamaica?' she asked him. 'Have you been here before?'

'I've worked all over the Caribbean,' Kyle smiled. 'In my younger, wilder days.'

'Worked? As a banker?'

'Mainly on yachts,' he answered.

Sophie's eyebrows rose. She glanced at him over Emma's head. 'Do tell.'

'Not likely,' he said easily. 'My disreputable past isn't a fit topic for the breakfast table. Besides,' he added with a glint, 'everyone needs a little mystery.'

'*Touché,*' she nodded, amused.

When Emma's ackee arrived Sophie sampled it, and found it every bit as delicious as Kyle had promised. After breakfast, the three of them went down to the beach.

It was another glorious morning, the sun blazing down from a cloudless sky. Sophie watched while Kyle swam, his muscular shoulders cutting an easy swathe through the surf. The child's presence had curtailed the rather dangerous flirtation that had been developing between them, which had been something of a relief. She was finding flirting with Kyle Hart to be a definite strain.

After a while Kyle emerged, dripping, and dried himself vigorously. Sophie couldn't take her eyes off him, fascinated by the way his body moved, the powerful muscles pulsing and relaxing in such perfect harmony. He was a man who would do everything to perfection, from dancing to making love...

He flopped down beside her on his back, closing his eyes with a sigh.

'This is the life. God, to think I have to go back to work some day!'

'It *is* rather hard to see you in a bank,' she admitted.

She pretended to be absorbed in her book, but she was really thinking about herself, about Maisie Wilkin, and about Kyle Hart.

Especially about Kyle.

He was magnificent, really. No wonder he had an oversized ego. And no wonder he'd been so contemptuous about Maisie. Beautiful people tended to be very unkind about those not so favoured as themselves.

But such shallowness deserved punishment. He shouldn't be allowed to get away with such a callous attitude. Somehow, she knew she could turn the present situation round to get her own back.

Somehow...

Last night, after showering, she'd gone to stand on the balcony to look at the midnight sea, and she'd realised that if she wanted to she was in a position to deal a blow to Kyle's pride that would make up in some way, at least, for the blow he had dealt to hers.

The only question was how to deal it in the fortnight she had left on Jamaica.

Sophie turned her head slightly to study Kyle. In repose, his face was cruelly beautiful. No man had any right to be so damned beautiful. No man had any right to possess a figure like that.

His broad chest moved in a slow, tranquil rhythm as he dozed off in the sun. Beads of water glistened like pearls against the bronzed skin that was so fine for a man's. What would it feel like to reach out and caress that muscular throat, trace the way it met the bending curve of his collarbone, continue across those broad pectoral muscles to the dark, hard points of his man's nipples?

The idea was both exciting and frightening. Any woman would be half afraid to awake the animal in this man. His masculinity was so very formidable; it was evident in every movement, in his speech, in the crisp hair that started just below the arching wings of his ribcage, making its way across the tightly defined muscles of his stomach to the dark triangle of his Speedo.

She looked away, weird feelings turning her blood into ice, then into flame. Well, she'd once had a monumental crush on this man, and it was too soon to pretend that she felt indifference. In any case, very few female hearts would ever feel totally indifferent to Kyle.

Then what did she feel?

Avoiding the question, she moved her gaze to little Emma, who was adding another turret to the sand-castle she was building, far too close to the threatening waves. Poor kid. Sophie really hoped that she would still have a home to go back to once this holiday was over.

A larger wave than the rest suddenly came rippling up the beach, flooding Emma's sand-castle. With a squeak of dismay, she tried to protect her creation, but it was too late. The retreating water left only a shapeless lump where the castle had stood.

'Oh, *no!*'

Smiling, Sophie got to her feet, and went over to help Emma rebuild her palace. 'You'll have to make it further back from the sea,' she told the woebegone little girl. 'I know all the lovely moist sand is down here, but we'll carry it up in the bucket.'

In a few minutes, Emma was intently decorating the walls of a new, even bigger castle with sea shells. Sophie sat beside her, watching and giving advice.

As the topmost turret went into place, she nodded approval. 'What you need now is a Union Jack to fly from the top.'

Emma's eyes shone. 'Oh, that would be perfect! But I haven't got one.'

'I have.' Smiling, Sophie produced the little paper flag on its toothpick. 'It was on the breakfast table. When you said you were going to build a sandcastle, I knew you'd need it.'

Delighted, the child planted the flag on her battlements, and Sophie left her playing imaginary kings and queens in her palace and went back to her book.

As she settled down beside Kyle he turned his head lazily towards her, opening his eyes to smoky green slits.

'You're being very kind to the kid,' he said softly.

She shook the sand off her book. 'I like children. And Emma's a lovely little girl.'

'I was thinking of taking her to Dunn's River Falls this afternoon, in the car. It's a spectacularly beautiful place. You can climb up the waterfall from the sea, along a sort of a ladder of pools and shelves. You have to go in a bathing costume, of course, but it's quite an experience.'

'It sounds it.'

'Care to come?'

There was a silence after the casual invitation. Sophie found herself staring blankly at the surf, wondering just what the hell she was getting into. Why hadn't she told him, right away, who she was?

Then she shook away the feeling of doubt. Let him stay fooled. It would make the truth, when it came, all the more of a shock to his arrogant system!

'I might,' she said coolly. 'Can I tell you how I feel after lunch?'

Kyle's eyes were closed again, absurdly long lashes fanning his tanned cheeks. 'As you please. It isn't just your face that's familiar, you know,' he said in the same relaxed tone. 'It's your voice, too. Your voice reminds me of some other woman even more than your face does. I just can't think who.'

She sat very still. 'Have you known so many women, then?' she asked lightly.

'A few.' He rolled on to his stomach, catlike, and suddenly the tawny eyes were open, and staring into hers. She'd taken her dark glasses off, and the glowing stare seemed to reach deep into her soul, searching after the truth.

For a shuddering moment she felt totally certain that he knew exactly who she was. How could any woman hide anything from a man with eyes like that? Frozen, she waited for the recognition.

Then the passionate curve of his mouth moved in a wry smile, and he shook his head. 'Whoever you are,' he said huskily, 'I'm glad you're here. You make the morning beautiful.'

Sophie's fingers were shaking slightly as she reached for her sunglasses and started to put them on.

His long fingers stopped her, trapping her hand in his own.

'Don't put them back on,' he requested quietly.

'Why not?'

'Because your eyes are remarkable. Cool and grey and calm. Put up with the sun for a while. For my sake.'

She felt her cheeks flush as she withdrew her hand from his, and defiantly put the sunglasses back on. 'If I didn't know you were a respectable banker,' she said drily, 'I'd suspect you of trying to flirt with me, Mr Hart.'

'I'm too sensible to try anything like that, Miss Webb.' Denied the enjoyment of her eyes, he was watching her satin-smooth mouth, his lids hooded. 'You're not the flirtatious type.'

'No?'

'Definitely not. Flirtations are for shallow people. You are as deep as well-water. With you, only a profoundly passionate love-affair would be possible.'

She opened the book, a thick best-seller, and stared at the pages.

'And you?' she heard her own voice asking. 'Are you deep or shallow, Mr Hart?'

'Well,' he grinned, 'let's say I'm getting a little deeper with each year that passes.'

'But you're still shallow?'

'Better than I was. At your age, I certainly wasn't as grave and solemn as you are.'

She still didn't look up from her book. 'I'm not exactly a child.'

'How old are you? Twenty-two? Twenty-three?'

'Twenty-three.'

'I'm almost fifteen years older than that,' Kyle said gently. 'Yet you make me feel...daunted.'

'That's an odd word.'

'I'm always daunted by the inaccessible. You remind me of a teacher I had at infant school. Miss Willoughby, her name was. We called her Miss Willowy, because she was so slender and unapproachable. She had the same iceberg poise that you have.'

Sophie looked up at last. He was studying her figure with that provocative gaze, as though wishing that the one-piece costume wasn't there. His eyes dwelled on the scarlet V between her thighs, caressed her slim midriff, and took in the slight but definite curve of her breasts against the clingy metallic fabric. If he'd looked at his kindergarten teacher with those eyes, she thought wryly, turning slightly away from him, he had definitely been a precocious child!

'I'm sorry to hear that I daunt you,' she said, returning to her book, though she hadn't read a word of the last ten pages. 'But I wouldn't like to be thought of as too accessible.'

'You aren't,' he assured her, sunlight making her eyes smile like emeralds beneath their fringe of black eyelashes. 'The way you talk intrigues me, Sophie. You have the immaculate enunciation of a newscaster. No, not a newscaster... an actress.'

'How odd,' she said, trying to stop her expression from changing. 'I've never done any acting.'

'"I've never done any acting,"' he echoed her, his husky voice parodying her accent. 'You close your mouth so primly after every sentence, as though determined not to let any secrets out.'

'As you said earlier on, everyone needs a little mystery.'

Kyle laughed softly. 'Are you really reading that book?'

'It's extremely fascinating, as it happens.'

'It must be. You've just flipped two pages over at once, and you don't seem to have noticed.' He reached out and unstuck the two leaves that had clung together. 'There,' he said with a glint in his eye. 'Perhaps the story will make more sense now. If you've never tried acting, then you should do so. You certainly have the sex appeal and the beauty.'

'You think beauty is very important in a woman, don't you?' she asked drily.

'Well, isn't it?' Kyle smiled.

'It's a gift which very few women have.' She made no pretence of reading any more. 'Does that mean that you're only interested in those few women who *are* beautiful? Irrespective of what they're like as people?'

'You make it sound like a crime to admire a pretty face,' he laughed. 'As a matter of fact, I've always found that people who are lovable inside also possess a lovable exterior.'

'Now, that *is* shallow,' she retorted hotly. 'Beauty is an accident of birth. Possessing a good mind, or an upright nature, or kindness of heart—that isn't. By your lights, you would laugh at an ugly saint and admire a beautiful fraud!'

'I haven't ever seen a saint, ugly or otherwise,' he said, amused at her heat. 'But I would argue that intelligence, honesty or kindness of nature are just as much accidents of birth as beauty.'

'You're splitting hairs.'

'I don't think so. In any case, you're taking me far too simply. My views aren't as crude as you're trying to make out. Otherwise I would fall in love with a statue, like Pygmalion. A woman can have all the trappings of conventional good looks, but without the inner light to illuminate that mask she is not truly beautiful. She's pretty, but she's vapid and uninteresting.' His eyes met hers. 'That is what I meant. By the same token, a plain face can be made beautiful by the fire in the eyes, or the expression on the mouth.'

'You're confusing image with reality!'

'But how can you separate the two?' he challenged. 'My dear Sophie, I'm sorry if my compliments just now sounded patronising. When I said that you had the beauty to succeed as an actress, I meant that you had beauty in addition to a natural talent.'

'Now, how would you know whether I have any natural talent?' she asked him, her lips curling into a mocking smile.

'It's obvious. You're acting all the time.'

Her smile faded. 'I don't know what you mean.'

'Of course you know what I mean,' Kyle contradicted her calmly. 'Whoever or whatever you are, Sophie Webb, you're as well hidden behind your beautiful façade as a she-leopard sitting in the long grass. Or as any actress behind a role.' His eyes were as hard as diamonds, and, though he was smiling slightly, that cruel intentness was suddenly very disconcerting again. 'You accuse me of being shallow, of only being interested in your beauty. And yet, for some reason, you don't want me to get through to the real you, and you're devoting a lot of care to keeping me well away from whatever it is you hide behind those dark glasses.'

'You're lying right next to me,' Sophie pointed out, but her mouth was dry.

'In terms of getting near you, I might as well be lying somewhere on the other side of the world.' He shifted, sleek muscles coming into relief beneath his smooth skin, but he did not take his eyes from her face. 'No, you're an actress, all right. The best kind. The most elusive kind. You have that quality, that very special calibre, that either comes with years of experience or as a godsent gift.'

Sophie stretched her long legs, trying to maintain her casual pose. 'You sound as though you're something of an expert.'

'I enjoy the theatre. And I know several actresses. In fact,' he added, his eyes narrowing, 'you have a certain quality of one very fine actress, I know, Hélène le Bon…'

To her horror, his voice trailed off as he said the name, his stare fixed on her face with a concentration that made her heart suddenly leap into her throat. His mouth was half open, as though recognition was on the tip of his tongue.

For the second time in twenty minutes, she felt totally certain that the game was up. Then, out of her paralysis, she dredged up a languid tilt of the head.

'Hélène who?' she asked casually.

'Hélène le Bon,' he said slowly, a frown drawing his brows deep over his eyes.

'Oh, yes.' She made it sound utterly unconcerned. She sat up, turning her face away from him, and reached for the sun cream. As she smoothed the cool, sweetly scented stuff over her arms and shoulders, she said lightly, 'I've seen her in one or two things. She's very good. I'm flattered by the comparison, but I know you're really mocking me outrageously.'

She could sense his puzzled, fixed stare, and her heart was in her throat. She was certain that her skin had paled under her tan.

And then Emma came running over to them. 'Uncle Kyle! Come and see my palace!' She seized her uncle's hand, and started dragging him over to her sand-castle. With a wry smile he acceded, and the moment was broken.

Sophie started breathing again as he walked off with the child. Hell! There had been a damned sight too many close shaves so far! How long could she keep this little charade up?

She stared thoughtfully at Kyle's splendid figure as he examined Emma's castle. He was a hell of a lot more perceptive than she'd given him credit for. Though it was true he hadn't recognised her yet, despite a few close calls, he had very swiftly picked up the fact that she was concealing something from him. Given no more than the tiniest hint, she felt in her heart that he would see through her, once and for all.

She would have to be very, very careful. Kyle would have made an excellent interrogator, she thought, enjoying the jasmine scent of her sun cream. He observed with the keenness of a predator, and he let no slip pass unnoticed. There was a formidable intelligence behind that devastatingly male visage.

The closer he got to discovering her identity, the more determined she became to keep up the defence. She was enjoying this game intensely. Those moments when she'd thought he'd recognised her had been terrifying, yet had thrilled her to the core. Keeping him from recognising her had turned into a challenge every bit as stimulating as becoming Maisie Wilkin had been.

If he was really the connoisseur of acting that he'd said he was, she felt sure that he would appreciate the quality of the performance that she had put on, just for his benefit, over three Jamaican weeks.

But that was not to be until she willed it. She was determined that he should not discover her secret before she left the island, and determined that realisation should come in a way of her own choosing. Maybe she would suddenly be gone one morning, leaving him a mocking note, telling him who she really was and reminding him of how he had once found her so absurd.

Hmm, that was good.

She wanted to leave him with just a touch of the humiliation and anger he had once awoken in her.

She wanted to leave Kyle Hart grinding his beautiful white teeth!

CHAPTER THREE

NAKED in her bathroom after her shower that evening,
Sophie smoothed an after-sun gel all over her body. Ever
since coming here, she had been determined to take extra-
special care of herself, and the cooling, moisturising
lotion would give her skin an added lustre, replacing the
oils that exposure to the Caribbean sun would have
destroyed.

Sophie turned to the full-length mirror and studied
her reflection dispassionately. This holiday in Ocho Rios
was putting a fine gloss on her physique. She was a very
different woman from the one Kyle had known eight
months ago.

Not a trace of excess fat was left on her tall, slim
frame. Her face, which had tended to become moonlike
under the influence of three extra stones, was now a
delicate oval, framed by tawny-brown hair, curling after
a day of being constantly wet. Her breasts, too, which
had been puppyishly rounded in Brighton, were back to
their usual high curves. She'd always thought them far
too small, so slight that they hardly cast a shadow on
her ribcage, the rose-petal discs in their centres the only
sensual thing about them; but she'd been glad to shed
the unwonted heaviness, and to dispense with her B-cup
bras.

She turned, and studied her back view over her
shoulder. Trim bottom, long, elegant legs, a smoothly
lovely back that gleamed with the coating of lotion.
Already, she was tanned to the colour of burned honey,
and would have to be careful not to let her skin get too
dry.

Kyle was interested in her; she could say that without
vanity, and know it was true.

The afternoon had been marvellous fun. There had been no more nerve-jittering moments of recognition—the three of them had been having far too much amusement for that.

Ostensibly organised for little Emma's benefit, the trip to Dunn's River Falls had been a huge success. The place had been just as exquisite as Kyle had said it would be, a primevally lovely spot from the first dawn of creation. They'd all got soaked clambering up the cascades, wallowing in fresh-water pools, and discovering caves and grottoes where luxuriant ferns grew in abundance.

From there they'd driven up to Runaway Bay, where there were more caves to explore, romantic enough to have Emma squealing with excitement. By the time they'd got back the little girl was happily exhausted, declaring it to be the best day of her life.

It had certainly been one of Sophie's better days.

She'd felt Kyle's eyes on her all day. And once or twice, when he'd helped her up some particularly awkward spot, his strong hands had touched her body with a possessive appreciation that had set her blood racing.

He was certainly all man. If she was toying with him, then it was a dangerous game. And, like all dangerous games, it had both its perils and its rewards. Revenge in this case was going to be very sweet. She just had to be careful that she didn't burn her own fingers in the bright flame of her sport!

On the way back, he had casually invited her to spend the next day with them, describing an alluring trip round the island as bait. After an initial hesitation, she'd accepted. It was easy to tell herself that it was all part of her plan for revenge.

Well, not quite revenge, maybe. But retribution of a kind was certainly within her grasp.

Really, he had already walked into the trap so neatly that she didn't have to do a thing. The irony of it was so perfect that she was aching for someone to share it with. All she needed was the right moment to tell him

who she was, and to tell him that she'd overheard him
that afternoon on Brighton beach.

And then she could walk away from Kyle Hart, and
never think of him in her life again.

In the meantime, why should she feel any guilt about
abusing his trust or his hospitality? If he wanted to ap-
point himself as her personal guide to Jamaica, then let
him. By her calculations, he owed her a little atonement!

She dressed for dinner in a cool chiffon blouse with
a narrow grey skirt. One of the nice things about the
San Antonio was that its guests treated dinner as a dress-
up occasion, and, considering the excellent restaurant,
and the beautiful dining-room with its view of the bay,
there was no artificiality about that.

Kyle and Emma weren't in the dining-room; Kyle had
told Sophie that he would be dining with friends in
Kingston, and had taken Emma with him. He evidently
knew Jamaica well, and had many acquaintances on the
island. All to do with that shady past, no doubt.

So she ate alone, thinking about the afternoon, and
what it had felt like to be with Kyle Hart again.

It had felt very strange. There was a sense of *déjà vu*,
inevitably. Yet the fact that she knew who he was, but
he didn't know who she was, threw a strange spice into
the mixture. There was something oddly erotic about it
all. Why that should be, Sophie could not tell. But
somehow the situation was one she found exciting,
amusing, even sexy. Having got over the shock of seeing
him again, she was enjoying the strange feeling of being
half in control of events, half at the mercy of whatever
would happen.

She must be one of the few women, she thought with
a smile, to have ever stayed one step ahead of Kyle Hart!

'What would you like tonight, Miss Aspen?' Franklyn,
her favourite waiter, was beaming down at her, and she
smiled back at him. He was middle-aged and fatherly,
and had pampered her right from the start, always
making sure no one served her except himself.

'What do you recommend?' she asked.

'The seafood platter is extra good tonight,' he assured her. 'Good crayfish, fresh from Port Maria this afternoon. And lots of those prawns you like so much.'

'That sounds lovely, then.'

'Shall I call the wine steward?'

'No,' she decided, 'I'll stick with mineral water, thanks.'

He brought the splendidly presented platter a few minutes later. As she was becoming something of a pet of the Jamaican staff, the dishes she got tended to be a little special, and tonight was no exception.

'Wow!' she gasped at the array of shellfish. 'I'll never get through all that!'

Franklyn took the silver lobster-crackers and dealt with the crab's claws for her. 'I see you been makin' friends with Mr Hart and his little girl.'

'Well, we got talking,' Sophie said, not rising to the bait.

'Mighty fine-lookin' man,' Franklyn said, dealing efficiently with the hard shells. 'Knows Jamaica pretty well, so they say. Used to live here.'

'Do they? What else do they say?'

'They say Jamaica knows *him* pretty well,' Franklyn grinned.

'What does that mean?'

'Means he's a popular man with the ladies.' Franklyn straightened and started serving up the food. 'Got an eye for a pretty face. Which I guess is why he so interested in you, Miss Aspen.'

Sophie looked up quickly. 'He's been asking you about me?'

'This morning,' Franklyn confirmed, dark eyes twinkling. 'Seen me talkin' to you last night, and I guess he thought I could fill in a few details for him. Seemed to think your name was Miss Webb.'

Sophie bit her lip. 'Did you . . .?'

'I didn't tell him no different,' Franklyn said with a chuckle. 'In fact, I didn't tell him a thing about you. Just that he was the tenth feller to have asked about you in a week!'

'Thank you for not giving the game away, Franklyn.' Sophie sighed. She struggled to find an adequate explanation for her deception of Kyle. 'You see, I'm playing a sort of joke on Kyle Hart——'

'You don't need to explain a thing, Miss Aspen.' He put the immaculate napkin over his arm, and beamed down at her. 'But I tell you one thing—you got that gentleman bamboozled.'

'What does that mean?'

'Reckon he's heading into the lobster-pot as sure as that old crayfish there on your plate.'

Seismically amused by his own wit, Franklyn glided away from her table.

Sophie was awakened the next morning by a persistent tapping on her door. Wrapping herself in her lightweight gown, she went yawningly to open it.

Emma's eager face looked up at her shyly. 'You haven't forgotten? You promised you'd come!'

'I hadn't forgotten,' Sophie smiled, shaking her tousled head. 'Where's your uncle?'

'Getting dressed,' Emma replied. It was just eight. She was all ready for the day's excursion, a wide-brimmed straw hat perched on her dark hair, and her pretty little face alight with excitement.

'OK,' Sophie said, stifling another yawn. 'I won't be long. Want to come in while I get ready?'

The child nodded, and Sophie let her in. She hopped on to Sophie's tumbled bed, chattering joyously as Sophie went into the bathroom and stepped into the shower.

'We're going to dig for treasure,' she announced. 'And then we're going to dive for pearls. And then we're going to eat crayfish...'

Sophie smiled to herself as she listened to the recital through the spray of her shower. She was looking forward to the day, though her expectations weren't as sanguine as Emma's.

She washed her slim body, dried herself, and got straight into her costume. Like yesterday's, it was a one-piece, but this time in stretchy mauve Spandex, clinging to her form with flattering sexiness. It was really a little too revealing, but it gave her a kind of wicked pleasure to parade in front of Kyle the wares he'd once held in such contempt!

She went back into the bedroom to finish dressing.

'You've got such lovely clothes,' Emma sighed. At eight, she was already alert to fashion, and loved bright colours. 'My mum wears pretty things, too.'

'Does she?' Sophie asked, stepping into a deep blue sun-dress and zipping it up.

'Yes. Mum and Dad are talking about getting divorced, you know.'

Sophie tried not to wince at the blunt announcement. 'Oh. I'm sorry to hear that.'

'That's why Uncle Kyle's taking me on this holiday. I'm not supposed to know. But I do.'

Sophie put some underwear, a sun-dress and an extra towel in her basket, along with an assortment of toiletries, sunglasses, hairbrushes and general feminine accoutrements. 'I suppose you couldn't help knowing about something like that,' she said slowly.

'They might be divorced by the time I get back.' Emma obviously had a rather vague idea of what was involved, which was just as well. She looked relatively unconcerned. 'My best friend's mum and dad got divorced last year. Lots of the girls at school have got divorced mums and dads, too.'

'Well, let's hope it doesn't happen to you,' Sophie smiled. 'Think you can wait while I do my hair in a plait?'

'I'll help,' Emma offered. 'I always help Mummy do hers.'

'OK.' Sophie got on the bed next to her, and sat cross-legged while the girl busied herself with the thick chestnut hair at the back of her head.

'Do you like your Uncle Kyle?' she asked.

'Oh, he's *fabulous*!' Emma enthused. 'He's the hand-somest man in London.'

'Is he?' she replied, amused.

'Don't you think so?'

'I've seen worse, I guess. He seems very fond of you, for some unknown reason, too.'

Emma giggled. 'Daddy says he used to be the black sheep of the family, but not any more. What *is* the black sheep of the family?'

'You'll have to ask your Uncle Kyle that,' Sophie hedged discreetly.

'And Mummy says he should get married and settle down. Except,' she added, 'he hasn't found the right woman yet.'

Sophie tried to hide her smile. It was odd to hear these scraps of grown-up conversation coming out of Emma's mouth. 'And did you have a nice time last night?'

'Oh, *yes*!' Emma enthused. 'We went to some friends of Uncle Kyle's. There was music and dancing, and a feast——'

'A feast?'

'That's what they call it in Kingston. Where the food's all laid out, and you sort of help yourself.'

'A buffet?'

'I think so. It was scrummy, anyway.'

'Lots of pretty ladies wearing lovely clothes?' Sophie probed.

'Mmm! There was a *super* Jamaican lady dancing with Uncle Kyle. She looked like a model. Not like you, though. Different.'

'Prettier?' Sophie asked casually.

'Well...' Diplomacy struggled with accuracy as Emma concentrated on the plait she was making. 'Maybe just a tiny bit. She was ever so tall and smart, with a lovely figure. She had beautiful hair, too, done in sort of an Afro style. Like in the films.'

'I see.'

'Her name was Francie. She and Uncle Kyle go way back.'

'Oh, they do, do they?' Sophie commented, feeling the flame of jealousy flutter into life. 'Did he dance with this beautiful Francie all night?'

'I don't know,' Emma answered with devastating honesty. 'I got put to bed at ten. But he seemed very fond of her. Is that all right?'

Tying the plait, Sophie checked in the mirror. It was surprisingly proficient, and gleamed glossily at her nape. 'That's lovely,' she smiled. 'Let's go!'

They went downstairs to the car, where Kyle was already waiting, wearing figure-hugging denims and a loose tank-top. He greeted her with a grin, and Sophie found herself wondering rather bitterly whether Francie with the lovely figure and Afro hair was responsible for a certain cat-that-got-the-cream air about Kyle this morning.

'Did you sleep well?' he asked.

'Very well,' she nodded. The impact of Kyle's beauty was hitting her all over again. His tan was deepening visibly after days in the sun, and in the denims that hugged his hips and the crisp cotton shirt he looked anything but a banker from London. More like a Hollywood sex symbol doing a bit of beach-combing.

He took her hand and lifted it to his lips. The light kiss gave her a shivery sensation of goose-flesh.

'Blue suits you well,' he said, studying her calmly. 'You look stunning. You could pose for Aphrodite rising from the foam.'

'Thank you, kind sir,' she said, and cursed herself for the blush that rose to her face.

Kyle opened the door for her, amusement registering on his bronzed features.

'You're not very poised for a top model,' he said. 'Aren't you used to compliments?'

'You say things that are just outrageous. They aren't compliments.'

Getting into the convertible, Sophie was having the weirdest feeling. It was exactly like being a young family, going on a glamorous outing together. Except that she wasn't married to the man, and the child wasn't theirs.

They set off inland, and drove across the centre of the island towards Mandeville, a hilltop town of cool English elegance. Its white houses were dazzling in the morning sun. Pausing there to wander along the Georgian avenues, and to buy Emma a glass of iced coconut-milk, they headed on towards the coast and Treasure Beach.

The vast sweep of golden sand, fringed on one side by a sea of impossible blue, and thick tropical vegetation on the other, was an incredibly beautiful sight. Sophie was enchanted, but Emma, clutching her spade and bucket, looked dismayed.

'But where's the treasure *buried*?' she wailed.

'That's for you to find out,' Kyle smiled. 'I didn't say it was going to be easy, did I?'

'It could be anywhere!'

'You never know your luck,' Kyle said solemnly. 'And I've got a clue. The treasure is buried under the biggest palm tree on the beach.'

'It must be that one! Or that one!'

'Well, let's cool off with a swim before you start digging,' he suggested.

The sand was already burning hot as they walked down to the sea across the dunes, and Sophie couldn't resist the delicious turquoise water. As soon as they'd found a satisfactory place to settle, she pulled off her shorts and shirt and ran into the sea.

The water was ravishingly cool as it flooded round her body. She struck out towards the horizon, splashing blissfully. It was a perfect day. The sky overhead was a vault of sapphire-blue, the sunlight pouring down like gold. Kyle and Emma followed her. He was completely at home in the water, moving with the easy grace of a big fish. He smiled at Sophie, the deep blue of the sky reflected in those green eyes, turning them the colour of the sea.

'You look as though you're enjoying yourself.'

'I love Jamaica,' Sophie sighed rapturously. 'I just know I'll come back some day.' They swam for almost an hour, just revelling in the sea and the natural beauty all around them.

When at last they were lying in the baking sun, with Emma digging hopefully for treasure under the biggest palm tree she could find, Kyle turned to her.

'When are you thinking of leaving Jamaica?'

'I don't know,' she answered idly.

'Don't you have a job to go back to?' Kyle probed. 'No assignment waiting for you back home?'

'Not for the moment,' she replied.

'Does that mean I have you to myself on an indefinite basis?' he asked, the smile warm in his voice.

'You don't have me to yourself on any basis,' she replied tartly. She looked up. He was watching her. Once wet, the mauve Spandex costume clung to her in a very revealing fashion, and he wasn't bothering to disguise his interest in her anatomy. She fought down her prudish instinct to cover up. After all, she enjoyed looking at his body. Why should she feel so awkward? Stop being Maisie, she warned herself, and remember that you're Sophie again!

A beaming Jamaican beach vendor had arrived, with a vast basket of fruit balanced on her head. Kyle bought them bananas, pineapples and some strange, knobbly looking things that were called sweet-sop. He washed the pineapple in the sea, and started peeling it with a knife.

'What about you?' she asked, watching him carve the dripping fruit. 'How long are you planning on staying here?'

'I'm in no hurry to leave,' he said, his eyes holding hers. 'But if my brother and his wife take a long time sorting out their marriage, I'm thinking of chartering a yacht, and taking Emma across to Haiti and the Dominican Republic. To the Cayman Islands as well, if we have the time. Maybe even to Cuba.'

'Not exactly the well-beaten tourist track,' Sophie remarked, glancing at him.

'No,' Kyle agreed. 'But it's worth it, just for the Creole cooking.' His smile glinted in the sunlight as he sliced the golden pineapple into juicy rounds. 'Besides, I know those islands well enough to be able to take care of myself—and Emma.'

'Knowledge gleaned during your misspent youth?'

'Mmm.'

She assessed the powerful muscles of his chest and shoulders from under her thick lashes. 'You're very discreet about that misspent youth of yours. Was it so very wicked?'

'Well, I wasn't always a dull pen-pusher, slaving away in a City bank,' he said in amusement.

'So what took you to the Caribbean?'

'It's a long story.'

'We've got all morning,' she hinted. He passed her some pineapple, and she bit into the fruit. It was nectar, with none of the acidity she associated with pineapples in England.

'Nice?' he asked, watching her.

'Heavenly.' She was getting the juice everywhere, but with the sea two steps away who cared? She brushed her chin with the back of her wrist. 'But I want to hear about why you came to Jamaica.'

'Well, the essence of it is that my father is one of the directors of a merchant bank in London. It isn't a very big one,' he smiled, catching her expression, 'but it's very well established, and it has a good name in the City. It's been going for a hundred and thirty years.' He consumed a chunk of pineapple, making a neater job of it than she had done. 'The tradition in our family is that the eldest son always goes into the bank. I happen to be the eldest of the three of us, but when I came out of university I just wasn't ready to go into servitude.'

'Poor thing,' she condoled in a voice like lemon drops, 'born to such a dreadful fate. Fancy having wealth and a distinguished career thrust upon you so cruelly.'

He laughed huskily. 'I didn't see it quite like that at the time.' He passed her another piece of fruit. 'All I knew was that people who worked in banks were dull and staid and grey. I had the idea that bankers just sat around counting money all day. Well, I was crazy about yachts and yachting, and all I wanted to do was see the world. I told my father that I needed two years to settle down, and he reluctantly agreed. So I took off.'

'How, exactly, took off?'

'I got a job, crewing on a yacht bound for Montego Bay. When I arrived, I just fell in love with the place.'

Sophie smiled, and hummed from 'Jamaica Farewell'. 'I took a trip on a sailing ship, and when I reached Jamaica, I made a stop.'

'Exactly,' he laughed. 'I spent the next twenty-six months in the Caribbean, mainly working on yachts between the islands. Sailing and . . . seeing life.'

'Was she dark-skinned or light-skinned?' Sophie enquired, deadpan.

Kyle laughed softly. 'There were two, actually, and both had skins the colour of *cortado*—what the French call *café au lait*. They taught me a great deal about life...and love. But they weren't the only reason I stayed. I really did come to love the Caribbean. The work was hard, but I was fit and ready for most things.'

He didn't need to elaborate. Wisely, Sophie resisted the impulse to ask whether one of the ladies had been called Francie. 'It sounds like fun.'

'Life was good,' he agreed. 'There was a lot of hard physical work, but I didn't have many responsibilities or worries. I was just living from day to day, doing what I loved. I had a lot of good times. Then, one time, we went up to Florida on a fishing trip, and I found a rusty old steel-hulled yacht for sale in a mooring in Miami. I had just enough money to buy her. I sailed her back to Kingston, and cleaned her up, begging and stealing the paint and varnish where I could. A month later, I went into the charter business.'

Sophie couldn't stop herself from smiling. 'Trust you. The mercantile genes were coming out, despite the attempt to break free.'

'There's more truth in that than you know,' he agreed. 'It must have been my destiny.'

'What astrological sign are you?' she asked.

Kyle snorted. 'You don't believe in all that silliness, do you?'

'I don't knock it,' she replied. 'You talked about destiny just now, didn't you? So tell me, what sign are you?'

'Scorpio.' He gave her a dry look. 'Now you're going to tell me I'm ambitious, vindictive and deeply passionate, right?'

'I wouldn't know,' she smiled, 'but those are typical Scorpio characteristics. Especially the vindictive bit. Most Scorpios I've known have been great ones for getting their own back. Their motto seems to be "don't get mad, get even"!'

'Could be true,' he shrugged. 'I hate anyone to get one over me.'

'There you are, then. Do you always get your own back?'

'Always,' he said with a glint. 'Preferably in spades.'

Sophie felt a slight chill touch her skin, despite the tropical sun. But Kyle was smiling easily. 'And you?' he asked. 'Where do you come in the zodiac?'

'I'm a Virgo.' Somehow, that made her blush stupidly, and his keen eyes didn't miss that fact.

'That suits you rather well,' he smiled. 'Didn't I say you had a cool, touch-me-not quality? So—what happens when a passionate, ambitious Scorpio male meets a cool, vestal Virgo female?'

That was not a question she cared to go into! 'We were talking about your misspent youth,' she reminded him firmly. 'What happened after you got into the charter business?'

He sighed. 'Well, it was the beginning of the end, of course. I went at it with all my enthusiasm. In six months, I was buying two more yachts and starting to hire my own crews, and six more months later my bank manager was starting to talk about the benefits of floating a company.'

'Sounds like everybody's dream,' Sophie commented.

'It wasn't *my* dream.'

'The magic had worn off?'

'Unfortunately,' he nodded. 'While I was just lazing around, making love and having fun, it was paradise. Once money came into it, everything changed. I found I was thinking about the business all day long. Where I used to be content lying on the beach with a bottle of rum and a girl in my spare time, now I was making plans, working on boats, adding up figures.' He smiled at Sophie gently. 'One morning, I woke up, and I realised I was out of my place. I could be doing the same work in the bank, and that was where I belonged.'

'Just like that?'

'I discovered that I wasn't doing what I wanted any more. I was twenty-three, just your age, and I was playing truant from my real life.'

'Did you sell up?'

'Lock, stock and barrel. I was a little late on my promise to my father, but by the time I was twenty-five I was working in the bank, and heading for a seat on the board.'

She watched his face. 'And did you miss Jamaica?'

'On grey, drizzly days, yes. But I'd realised by then that I had sown my wild oats, and that responsibility couldn't be avoided for ever. But I've always been able to come back for holidays—though if I didn't have Emma,' he added with a glitter, 'I'd be staying somewhere very different from the San Antonio.'

'With one of your *café au lait* charmers?' she suggested, tilting a dry look at him.

'Somewhere like that,' he agreed easily. He evidently took no trouble to disguise the fact that he was footloose and fancy-free as far as women were concerned. 'As a matter of fact,' he went on, 'I learned a lot in the Caribbean, about myself, and about business. And one of the things I'd picked up was that work doesn't have to be dull.'

'I assume you've added your own particular style to merchant banking?' Sophie asked.

He smiled faintly. 'In a way. My speciality is financing projects which other banks have rejected as too avant-garde, or too risky, but which I think are basically sound. Ninety-eight per cent of the time it pays off handsomely.'

'And the other two per cent?'

'The other two per cent has to be explained away to the board...very convincingly.' He smiled into her eyes. 'But I can be very persuasive.'

'I'm sure you can.' Her eyes dropped to the curve of his mouth, so temptingly male. 'So how do you judge the sound projects from the cranky ones?'

'Instinct.'

'Did you also learn how to judge the worth of people while you were sowing your wild oats in the Caribbean?'

'That,' he said gently, 'is the most difficult art of all. But I think I'm good at it.'

She raised an ironical eyebrow. 'Really? And you never go wrong, say...make a snap judgement on the face value of things?'

'We all do that, from time to time. But I try not to.'

'That must be a great talent,' she said with well-veiled sarcasm.

'Why do I have this idea that you're laughing at me all the time?'

'Why should I laugh? Your life has evidently been a mixture of Errol Flynn and Pierpont Morgan.'

He laughed out loud at that, throwing his head back. He was so handsome that he made her heart ache. 'You're an ironical creature,' he observed, meeting her eyes in amusement. Laughter was still rumbling in him as he rose to his feet. 'I'd better go and make sure Emma finds some treasure.'

'Have you brought something?'

He showed her a little silver ring, set with a 'ruby'. It was clearly inexpensive, but quite authentically antique-looking all the same. 'I bought that from one of those Rastafarian stalls. Think she'll like it?'

'She'll adore it,' Sophie nodded.

'I think the kid needs a little spoiling.' He looked down at her, tall and tanned. 'I'm not much good at entertaining little girls, but I'm learning from you. I don't know how I would have managed if you hadn't been here.'

'She's not entirely unaware of what's going on at home,' Sophie said, wiping her sticky hands. 'She told me this morning that her mum and dad were talking about a divorce.'

Kyle's face changed. 'Damn. How do you stop a child from picking up these things?'

'You can't.' They looked at each other for a moment in silence. 'Have you heard from her parents yet?'

'My sister-in-law rang last night,' Kyle nodded. 'Things aren't going too well.'

'I'm sorry to hear that,' Sophie said.

'Yes. Well, it's just one of the things that happen, isn't it?' The bitterness on his face told her how much he cared, really. He walked across the beach to plant the ring in Emma's excavation.

Sophie went down to the sea to wash her hands. He was a strange man. So caring in some ways, so hard and ruthless in others. She basked in the sun for an hour, almost dropping off to sleep while Kyle entertained his niece. At noon they went back to the car, heading on down the coast towards Black River.

It was now fiercely hot. At a roadside stall they bought crabs and crayfish roasted over the coals, together with 'bammies', manioc bread, and stopped in a particularly scenic spot to eat their feast. The food was delicious and fresh, given added zest by being eaten in the open, in such glorious weather. Emma was bubbling with delight over her ring, apparently completely unsuspecting that it hadn't been lying in the sand since Captain Morgan's time.

At Frenchman's Reef, they swam again, this time wearing face masks, and using snorkels. The water was clear and calm, and though they didn't find any pearls the underwater scenery was weirdly beautiful, bright shoals of fish flickering through miniature forests of corals, and waving fields of sea-grass patching a submarine landscape of pure silver sand.

In the late afternoon they drove on to Bloody Bay. All day they had been getting further and further from the well-beaten tourist areas, and now they were in almost completely unspoiled countryside. The wide and empty scenery had exerted a powerful hold on Sophie, and she was realising how much she'd missed by staying around Ocho Rios. Bloody Bay had an even longer beach, and even warmer water, than Treasure Beach.

After a final swim, Emma curled up in the shade of a sand-dune and fell asleep, while Kyle took Sophie on a gentle ramble along the water's edge.

The relationship between them had been growing more warm and intimate all day, and now they just walked in silence, not talking much, just sharing the beauty of the day and the landscape.

'It really is extraordinarily lovely,' Sophie sighed at last, as they stopped and looked back along the shimmering sand. The warm, lapping sea had all but obliterated their footprints. They were the only two solitary figures in all the vast beauty of sea and sand.

'You fit in well,' he said softly, 'because you're an extraordinarily lovely woman. I find it hard to believe that you're not surrounded by a coterie of pursuing men,' he went on. 'You must have left them in England.'

'No, there's no one in England.'

'Not a soul?'

'There are always men in my life,' she said, meeting his eyes briefly. 'But not in the sense you mean.'

'What sense do I mean?'

'Well, I presume you're asking me whether I have a lover,' she smiled.

'And the answer is no?'

'Not at the moment.'

'A true Virgo?' Kyle was looking at her with an expression that made her heart suddenly clench in reaction. He was wearing only faded denims, his powerful torso naked to the sun. She, in her mauve one-piece, with a frayed straw hat shading her eyes, looked captivatingly graceful and feminine.

'You're exquisite in this light,' he said in a quiet voice.

She tried to laugh the comment off, and turned away. Despite her daily swims and exercise, she was feeling pleasantly tired. She couldn't match the power of that hard body of his. 'My legs are aching exquisitely, at any rate.'

'How else could exquisite legs ache?' he smiled. 'I must have worn you out with all that swimming and walking.'

'I'm not as strong as you are,' Sophie pointed out. 'I've loved it—I just feel a bit the way Emma does.'

'I ought to be shot. Let's go and sit on the sand over there.'

They walked over, and settled down in the lee of the breeze that had sprung up. The sand was warm, radiating back the heat of the day. With a sigh of bliss, Sophie lay back against its soft, yielding warmth, and closed her eyes. 'To think that all this has to end,' she said dreamily. 'It doesn't seem fair. Beauty should never have to end.'

She felt his fingers touch her hair, caressing the salt-stiffened tangle gently. She half opened her lids languidly, looking up at him with eyes that had taken on the colour of the evening sky.

'This is what I like about you,' he said.

'My awful hair?' she smiled.

'Your beautiful hair,' he corrected. 'The way you don't fiddle and fuss with it all the time. I like women to be natural. I hate that neurotic, twitchy way some women behave.'

She thought of the way her fiddling with her glasses had irritated him in Brighton. He was leaning over her, smiling down at her, and at that moment she felt very close to him, and that she wanted him very much.

'Is it a cliché to say that you're radiant?' Kyle asked. His fingers trailed down the satin-smooth skin of her cheek to trace the delicate arc of her jawline. 'Your skin is the colour of gold, yet it's got an almost pearly quality, finer than the finest silk that was ever spun.'

'The afternoon has gone to your head,' she said, trying to ignore the long fingers that were caressing her neck.

'Maybe,' he conceded. 'How are your legs?'

'Better.' His caresses were not having a soothing effect on her. His touch was deliberately sensual, yet as light as thistledown. 'We must have walked miles today.'

He did not answer, but bent slightly to touch her lips with his.

A touch, no more. The velvety warmth was there on her mouth, then gone. She felt her lips part, her eyes closing with the reaction that had swept across her skin.

'You've got goose-bumps,' he said softly, his fingers trailing down her arm where the fine golden hairs were erect. The extra-responsive condition of her skin made his touch something between torment and ecstasy. Sophie felt his lips touch her forehead, drifting down her eyelids.

The warm moistness of his tongue told her he was tasting the sea-salt on her temples, and she shuddered involuntarily. She was in the grip of a kind of sweet hypnosis, immobile in the warm sand while Kyle kissed her face, his mouth never touching hers, drawing close, then moving away with maddening deliberation.

When at last her lips touched his, Sophie knew that it had been by her own movement. She lifted her full, sensitised mouth to his, and felt him kiss her there at last, his arm sliding round her to draw her close.

Her lips clung to Kyle's, possessed of a will of their own. His tongue traced the shape of her soft lower lip, touching her white teeth, meeting the sensitive tip of her own tongue. His lips pressed harder as passion took the place of exploration. He was tasting the deep inner secrets of her mouth for a dizzy moment; then he drew away, as though trying to discipline them both.

'I've been dying to do that all day,' he whispered.

He kissed her cheeks, her delicate eyelids, his mouth moving down her throat to find the scented hollow where her pulses fluttered madly.

She couldn't stop the soft moan of desire from escaping her parted lips. She had hungered for Kyle for so long, and this moment was so sweet. It was happening at last, the impossible dream she had ached for long ago...

Her slim arms slid around his neck, pressing his face to her throat, her neck arching as she felt the harsh touch of his teeth.

Who was conquering whom? She felt his palm caress her ribs, drawing closer to the gentle swell of her breast, where the skin was already tightening in reaction. His touch was possessive, yet thrilling. She was melting inside, her adoring heart starting to fail her.

Kyle whispered her name, his hand sliding into the V of her bathing costume to stroke the silky skin of her breasts. The sensation was so much more erotic than she could ever have dreamed. His touch was tender, yet accomplished; he knew how to touch a woman. She moaned aloud as his palm caressed the sultry tips of her nipples, drawing them into concentrated stars of aphrodisiac passion. His very gentleness was tormenting. The sensitive areas of her body were starting to throb with hunger, and Sophie felt her self-control start to slip.

With a supreme effort she drew away from him and unclasped her hands from round his neck.

'We'd better get back to Emma,' she said, in a voice that shook slightly. 'And we'd better stop what we're doing right now.'

'Why?' he wanted to know, smiling down at her with smoky eyes. His fingers eased aside the stretchy mauve top of her costume, revealing the paler curve of her breast, the rosebud tip tight and demanding at the centre.

The dark expansion of his pupils registered the way her nakedness had affected him; then, obeying the tacit demand, he bent his head, his mouth closing over her nipple.

Sophie gasped at the intimate kiss, his tongue feeling as rough as a cat's against her tender skin.

She ran her palms shakily over his powerful shoulders, up his neck. His hair was thick and crisp under her fingers as she drew his head down, wanting him to touch her harder, more fiercely. Kyle's teeth closed around the aroused flesh of her nipple, the caress becoming almost cruel. The pleasure was wickedly intense, drawing a whimper from deep in her throat. His hand was finding her other breast, seeking her other nipple, making forked lightning dart along her nerveways into her loins, turning desire into quivering hunger.

Unable to bear it now, Sophie arched away, and pulled the soft material of her costume back over her naked breasts. Suddenly the Spandex seemed a painfully flimsy protection, her aroused nipples making flagrant peaks against the mauve material.

'Please,' she begged, her eyes misty, 'if you respect me, don't touch me any more.'

He stared at her, his expression unmistakably desirous. 'Are you deliberately trying to drive me crazy?' he asked huskily. 'I want you, Sophie! Don't you know how I feel about you?'

'I know that I don't know you well enough to let you do this to me,' she replied, sitting up. Her mouth was dry with passion. 'Secondly, this isn't the time or place for what you feel, and thirdly, there's a little girl all alone over there——'

'Emma's quite safe.' He tilted his head to kiss her mouth again, and she felt the world spin around her. 'God, I want you,' he murmured, drawing her close.

'Kyle, don't——'

'You're so lovely,' he whispered raggedly. 'So slender and graceful, so cool and elusive...' His hand was caressing her hip, the satiny skin of her thigh. 'From the moment I saw you, I've been burning for you. And I know you feel the same way, too.'

'You don't know anything of the kind,' she retorted. But she had to speak between his kisses, and the blood was rushing in her veins, like molten gold being poured into a new mould, a new shape.

Kyle's hand slid into the smooth coolness between her thighs, caressing the delicate skin, so close to the aching, melting centre of her need that the slightest movement would be fatal.

His mouth claimed hers with hungry intensity, and then she felt his palm cup the mound of her womanhood, only the soft material coming between his possessive touch and her arousal.

Her eyes widened, her whole body tensing like a coiled spring at the feelings he was unleashing in her.

Then she remembered Maisie. Before he could stop her, she slid away from him, rose to her slender, shaky legs, and ran down the moist sand to the sea.

The warm water enveloped her, too warm and too salt to do much in the way of rinsing away her emotions, but at least she had escaped from the drowning maelstrom of Kyle's lovemaking.

For the time being.

Kyle followed her after a few moments, his magnificent face looking partly amused, partly frustrated. She was expecting some acid comment at the way she'd chickened out, but he didn't say anything to her, just swam beside her in silence until she was ready to get out again.

'We'd better set off,' he said, as they walked, both dripping, back to where Emma lay sleeping. 'It's a long drive back to Ocho Rios.'

'Yes,' she said flatly.

'Are you angry about what's just happened?' he asked, sliding a strong arm around her waist and pulling her close.

'No,' Sophie said, rather tensely. 'But I don't want it to happen again.'

'Oh, Sophie,' he said, in mock reproof. 'You don't really think it's going to end there, do you?'

She didn't answer him.

But later, when she was alone, she could no longer pretend that it was all just a mischievous game any more. She'd wanted to let Kyle's misconception about her run. She'd wanted to play some kind of joke on him, to sting him back for the way he had once stung her.

Yet somehow it wasn't working out as simply and as neatly as she'd expected.

Kyle wanted her. There was no doubt about it any more. If her ambition was to be desired by the man who had once spurned her, she knew deep down that her wish was fulfilled.

There ought to have been a delicious enjoyment in that. This was a man who had once ridiculed her infatuation with him. And today he had held her in his arms, and had wanted to make love to her, right there on the beach. If she'd wanted, she could have had him...as her lover.

Enjoyment? Yes, after a fashion.

But there was pain, too. That old, sharp pain, reminding her so keenly of a certain evening in Brighton. The pain of feeling that he was only looking at her exterior. Only looking at her body. As though what lay inside her counted for nothing, as though all the feelings and emotions, the intelligence and the wit, were all irrelevant to looking good and dressing well.

What was worse: being humiliated because of her appearance, or being desired for it?

Damn him, she thought with quick hurt. Damn him for his triviality! If she'd once thought he cared about her, about what she was like inside, today would have been the happiest in her life, instead of a moment of acute, bittersweet irony.

And there were further problems. Mainly her own, that was. She ought to have known herself well enough to foresee just how deeply she would become enslaved by him. Enslaved? Yes. There was no other word.

Sophie knew her own feelings. They ran deep and strong. Though she'd never committed herself to any man in the full physical sense, she'd always known that when she did fall in love with a man it would be forever. She'd always cherished the old-fashioned ambition of having, in the same man, her only lover, husband and partner through life.

Maybe that was just the naïve conservatism of her rural Yorkshire upbringing. But it was a part of her, and she felt with deep pain that she could never survive a casual affair, not with Kyle Hart.

Kyle was by his own admission a roamer as far as women were concerned. He was hardly the forever kind.

How could she be sure that their relationship had any prospects other than those of a pleasurable holiday romance, which would end, on his part, with no possibility of anything deeper or further? She could not. All that lay in front of her, as far as she could now see, was pain.

What on earth was she going to do? She had already played this game for so long that it had gone too far to call the chips in.

If she told him who she really was, could she be sure that he wouldn't reject her completely? The thought that he would react with fury, or with disgust, terrified her. That Scorpio temper was something to fear. She was no slavish adherent of astrology, but somehow Kyle fitted the Scorpio bill very well indeed. If he was true to the type, he would react badly to having been duped, and that sting in the tail could be fatal. She could either have told him who she was right at the very beginning, or——

Or not tell him at all?

The temptation was so strong. On the one side she risked losing Kyle forever. On the other, she had the prospect of two more weeks of certain heaven.

Perhaps there was a way she could have her cake and eat it. If she could avoid a physical affair, if she could just keep it to the kind of happy friendship they'd had until this afternoon, then what harm was there in letting him remain ignorant about her identity?

The decision was made. She wouldn't tell him. Not until the very end. Then, if he really cared about her, it would all work out. And if he didn't—well, she would have had her three weeks of heaven.

CHAPTER FOUR

SOPHIE sat down at the dressing-table to put on her make-up, and stared at her own face in the mirror. The cool grey eyes looked back at her with a misty hint of melancholy, and the full, passionate mouth was touched with sadness.

It was her last night in Jamaica.

Three weeks of heaven had flown by so quickly, the happiest three weeks of her life. She had known love, excitement, had seen her most secret dream come true—that she would meet Kyle Hart again, and that he would be as attracted to her as he had once been repelled.

He still didn't suspect a thing. He didn't even know she was going tomorrow. She hadn't told him.

Lying on her bed, her tan suitcases were almost completely packed, bright summer colours peeping out from under the lids. The cupboards and shelves were empty. The taxi was booked to take her to the airport at seven-thirty tomorrow morning; the hotel bill was paid; she'd rung London to ask Mrs Flanagan, her cleaning lady, to air and clean the flat for her arrival tomorrow night. Tomorrow night she would sleep in London, and all this would be just a dream. Including Kyle Hart.

Everything had come to a focal point tonight.

They'd spent so many beautiful days together, sometimes just lying on the beach, talking and laughing with the intimacy of lovers, sometimes exploring Jamaica together, Kyle's expertise about the island making him a fascinating guide.

But they had never become lovers—not in the physical sense. She'd been so careful to avoid letting him kiss or caress her, knowing full well by now the devastating physical effect he could have on her. Though she knew

74

her reserve had frustrated him intensely, she had deliberately shied away from the sensual relationship she knew
he wanted so badly. For that, at least, she was now profoundly grateful.

She was wearing only a cotton wrap, and it had drifted
aside to reveal the curves of her neat, high breasts, with
their delicate tips.

In the afternoon, on the beach, Kyle had asked her
to have dinner with him tonight—not in the hotel, but
in a restaurant in Kingston that he claimed was un-
matchable—and she'd accepted.

Her plans for tonight weren't definite. It was her last
performance, though, and she was determined to play
it to the hilt!

She checked her watch. She'd sat here mooning so
long that she was already running fifteen minutes late.
If Kyle was on time, then he would be cooling his heels
in the foyer already. Well, let him! A little waiting
wouldn't hurt that massive male ego.

Her face didn't need more than a touch of lip-gloss
and a hint of eyeshadow to leap into glamorous defi-
nition. She darkened her lashes with mascara, and
brushed her chestnut hair as vigorously as she could bear.
Her hair was the only incomplete note; not in any de-
finable style, it tended to become a glossy chaos of curls
and waves. But it was not an unattractive chaos, and it
would have to do.

She touched her wrists and the valley between her
naked breasts with a Giorgio Armani perfume, a
fragrance she had discovered recently, and which captivated her with its mysterious seduction.

Letting the wrap drift to the floor, she stepped into a
pair of lacy silk briefs, pulling them up over her slender
hips, then she lifted the dress off the chair where she'd
left it.

It was the only garment she had which was really
suitable for an occasion like tonight. She'd bought it in
Kingston a few days ago, knowing at the time that she

would probably never wear it in London, but thinking of it as a souvenir. A plain black sarong dress in silk chiffon, it looked demure, apart from having no straps and leaving her tanned shoulders bare.

Until she took a step forward, when the slit in the front opened from ankle to the top of her thigh, revealing a devastating length of honey-coloured leg.

Half-amused at her own daring. Sophie fastened the dress and stepped into black high heels. Stockings, she guessed, weren't *de rigueur* in Kingston in summer. She didn't have any jewellery except cheap costume stuff, so she did without. A final glance in the mirror confirmed that she was looking just as she wanted to look. The image was right. He would be dazzled.

She picked up her little evening bag, and walked out of the room to meet Kyle.

She was exactly forty minutes late. He was waiting in the foyer, in a white jacket, with his hands thrust into the pockets of his black dress trousers. He looked magnificent enough to make her heart miss a beat, a sensationally male presence, radiating an animal aura of potency.

He also looked very impatient. In fact, his white teeth were biting into his tanned lower lip as he glowered across the palm-filled acres of cream carpeting, the green eyes smouldering under the dark brows.

Sophie stepped out of the lift, and walked towards him, keeping her expression neutral. This was probably the only time in her life she would walk across a room like this, dressed like this, to meet a man like Kyle Hart.

He turned and saw her, and his left wrist instinctively came out of his pocket, turning the diver's watch so he could tell her just how long she'd kept him waiting.

But his eyes did not leave her to consult the time.

Instead, they widened slightly as they took in her face, then drifted down her figure to watch the way her right leg parted the black silk chiffon as she walked.

And one thing her experience as a model had taught her was how to walk across a room.

'Hello,' she said as she reached him, and gave him a cool smile. 'Isn't it a warm evening?'

'Uh—very warm,' he agreed, as though still trying to come to terms with her appearance. 'Sophie, you look...'

She tilted an eyebrow at him. 'Yes?'

'Come on,' he said, shaking his dark head slightly. He didn't mention that she'd kept him waiting for the best part of an hour, though Sophie guessed that he was the kind of man who didn't usually let things like that ride!

As he opened the passenger-side door of the white convertible to let her in, he touched the cool skin of her arm.

'Sophie,' he said quietly, 'you're utterly lovely.'

She settled into the seat, and looked up at him without missing a beat. The slim length of her thigh peeped through the silk. Kyle's almost tense expression told her how completely she had succeeded in her intention. She let a slight smile play across her mouth.

'Are you going to stand there all night, or shall we go and eat?'

He grinned, and leaned down to arrange the skirt so it covered her leg more demurely. 'That's a hazard to safe driving. Keep it covered if you want me to concentrate on the road.'

He closed the door, walked round the car, and got into the driver's seat. The roof was down, letting the balmy night air play around them.

'Top up or top down?' he enquired.

'Top down. It's hot.'

'OK.' He fired up the engine. 'Let's go.'

It was three-thirty in the morning, and the moon was a mother-of-pearl disc, high in the velvety dark blue sky, as they drove down the avenue of ghostly palm trees back to the San Antonio. In a very few hours, she would be on her way back to England.

But she didn't want to think about that.

Only now had the air started to cool down, and, after the evening they'd had, Sophie was glad to just lie back in the passenger seat and feel the crisp breeze caress her throat and shoulders. She raised her arms to lift her tumbled hair and let the cool wind get round the back of her neck, and sighed.

It had been a night of magic and enchantment. The restaurant he'd taken her to had been in the heart of downtown Kingston, the old part of the city. It had been the kind of place she'd never have dreamed of going to on her own, a dockside basement throbbing with reggae music and filled with an assortment of clients which had been, to say the least, picturesque.

But Kyle had been greeted as an old friend by the villainous-looking staff, and the meal they'd had—stuffed crabs, jerk pork cooked over pimento wood, yams, fried green bananas, and an exquisite pudding like a fruit fool, which Kyle had told her was called 'matrimony'—had been like nothing she'd ever eaten before. Washed down with lager, and concluded with rum and coffee, it had left her happily light-headed, a feeling which had persisted for the rest of the evening.

From there they'd moved on uptown to a nightclub with a terrace where they'd danced to the brilliant music of a calypso band. Kyle was being a charming companion, amusing her with the trenchant ease of a man who'd entertained a great many women in a great many different ways.

She hadn't tried to fool herself about her reaction to Kyle; he was sweeping her off her feet, and she loved it. She loved being held in his strong arms, losing herself in the bliss of snuggling up to his big, powerful body. Loved talking to him, listening to his pungently amusing conversation. Loved the fun he seemed to generate around himself.

He'd explained what some of the lyrics to the songs had meant, and they'd been wicked—and witty—enough to have her giggling helplessly.

Later, they'd gone on to a third locale, where they'd watched limbo dancing. The real thing. That had been very different from what had gone before, a pagan hint of voodoo accompanied by throbbing drums that spoke of dark magic and ancient ritual. Sophie had watched in taut fascination as the glistening, lithe brown bodies had performed almost impossible feats of agility, dancing beneath a flaming bar no more than a foot off the ground.

She'd been so sure some of the dancers would burn themselves that she'd found herself holding Kyle's hand tightly in her own. During one of the breaks, he'd kissed her. Nothing serious, just a gentle contact of lips, and yet the underlying message had been plain. A question, an invitation. A message that tonight didn't have to end.

'What are you thinking about?'

The question roused Sophie from her dreamy reverie. She curled in the seat to look at his profile.

'Tonight.'

'Have you enjoyed it?'

'Immensely.'

'We can do the same thing tomorrow night. And the next night, and the next...'

Sophie was silent, thinking of the packed suitcases lying on her bed, and the ordered taxi.

Suddenly, she was wishing that his promises were true—that her time here with Kyle was unlimited.

But that would only have been a consummation to be wished if she really had been an unknown to him, a mystery woman embarking on a holiday love-affair with a beautiful stranger.

As it was...

Earlier, he'd bought her a beautiful white gardenia from a street vendor, and now she touched the flower to her mouth, inhaling the sweet, exotic scent. 'Who is Francie?' she asked.

Kyle glanced at her, then smiled. 'Shame on you, to interrogate a child like that.'

'We girls have no secrets from one another. Was she one of your lovers when you lived in Kingston?'

'She's an old friend,' he hedged, his expression amused. 'You can't ask a gentleman to say more than that.'

They had arrived at the hotel. He parked the car, and they walked into the silent, beautiful foyer together. Apart from the night staff, the place was deserted.

Kyle turned to her, green eyes assessing. 'The bar's closed. So is the restaurant. Would you take it wrongly if I said I had a bottle of cognac in my room, and offered you a nightcap?'

Sophie considered him with a cool smile. 'How does one take an invitation like that rightly?'

'One accepts a gentleman's assurance that he won't try any funny business,' Kyle replied, holding her gaze. 'Despite the very considerable temptations.'

'Won't we disturb Emma?'

'Not unless you gulp your cognac very loudly. She's got the room next door, and there's a hotel baby-sitter with her.'

Sophie hesitated. She didn't want the evening to end, yet she was wary. It might be perfect to let it end here, and to be gone in the morning, leaving a letter for him at reception.

Then he smiled into her eyes, and caution melted into acceptance.

'I'd like a nightcap.' She nodded.

'Good.' He took her arm, and led her to the lift.

Kyle's room was bigger and more luxurious than her own, and the balcony commanded a spectacular view of the beach, and the moonlit sea that stretched out forever towards the horizon. She could hear the breakers rus-

tling far below, and smell the faint scent of some night-
blooming creeper.

He poured two brandies and brought them on to the
balcony. They toasted one another silently, and Sophie
sipped the fiery liquid.

Kyle tugged his tie off, and unbuttoned his collar.
Suddenly, with that V of tanned skin and dark, curly
hair showing, the pagan, animal quality in him was re-
inforced. He moved to stand beside her at the railings,
and stared out over the sea.

'It's so beautiful. On a night like this, I want to be
out at sea, on a yacht. The dark water beneath my keel,
a sail against the moon...and you, by my side.'

'What would I be doing there?' she smiled.

'What comes naturally. Don't be so cautious with that
cognac.'

'It's showing signs of going to my head.' She gulped
the liquid fire down, none the less, and felt its heat spread
through her system.

Kyle took the cognac glass out of her fingers, and put
it down. 'I know who you are, now,' he said softly.

Sophie's blood turned to ice, the heat of the cognac
going out like a quenched flame. 'You—know?' she
whispered.

'Mmm,' he nodded. 'You're the White Witch.'

Her breathing resumed. 'The White Witch?'

He smiled slightly. 'It's a local legend, but she really
once existed. Her name was Annie Palmer, and she came
to Jamaica in the 1820s, to marry the master of one of
the great estates, Rose Hall. She was young and beautiful, like you. But they said she was a witch. She certainly had a fatal effect on her three husbands, not to
mention her lovers.'

'Wow.'

'They always said she would come back. Maybe I'd
better get me a mojo,' he smiled, his eyes warm.

'What's that?'

'A hex to ward off a woman's spell.'

Sophie laughed rather breathlessly. Let that be the last close call she would have to deal with for a long time!

He drew her to him. 'Sophie...'

'A gentleman's promise,' Sophie said, laying a finger against his chest, to stop him getting any closer, 'ought to be inviolate. No funny business, you said.'

He looked down at her with brooding eyes. 'I can't get over that feeling that I know you from somewhere.'

It was time to go. 'You don't know me,' she said with a light smile, 'not from anywhere. It's been a lovely evening, Kyle. I won't forget it.'

'Neither will I.' He touched her cheek. 'One thing more. That trip to Haiti and Dominica I mentioned last week.' His eyes held hers. 'I want you to come with us.'

'Oh, Kyle——'

'I'm serious. It won't cost you anything, and if you haven't any work lined up at home, then you won't be missing anything.'

'Kyle, I can't——'

'We'll charter a yacht,' he cut through her protests. 'Haiti and Dominica are incredibly beautiful. They're fascinating places, with a unique art and culture. I'll take you to see real voodoo dancing—not the tourist stuff you saw tonight, but the authentic thing. We'll go to Sans Souci—I can promise you that you'll never see anything like it in your life again. If there's time, we'll go to the Caymans, where you can do some of the best diving in the world. The water at Spanish Bay Reef is crystal-clear—it's like drifting through the air.'

He had her hands in his now, and he was staring down at her with an almost pleading expression. 'Say you'll come, Sophie, and I'll start organising it tomorrow.'

'I can't say that,' she replied quietly. 'I hardly know you, Kyle. I can't commit myself to setting off with you on a yacht for an indefinite tour of the Caribbean. Not at four o'clock in the morning!'

'Then think about it,' he said forcefully. 'I'll start arranging a boat anyway, and you can give me your answer any time over the next few days. Is that agreed?'

'Nothing is agreed,' Sophie retorted, feeling painfully uncomfortable. She withdrew her hands from his. 'If you insist on making arrangements, then I can't stop you. But don't count on my coming with you. In fact, you might as well know here and now that it's extremely unlikely that I will come with you.' More unlikely than he knew, she added mentally.

'Why not?' he challenged. 'I'm promising you a little slice of heaven, and all you can do is shake your head.'

'My idea of heaven doesn't come in little slices.'

'What does that mean?'

'Oh, I don't know what it means,' she said restlessly, turning away from him. 'You're too sudden, Kyle. People just don't behave the way you want them to.'

'All I know is that you're having a very special effect on me,' he said quietly. She felt his hands take her arms and turn her to face him. He looked down intently into her face. 'There's something about you that tantalises me, eludes me. I don't really know what to do about it, but I want the feeling to stay.'

Sophie looked up at him, her heart starting to thud against her breast-bone. He drew her close, and kissed her parted lips with gentle force.

'Sophie,' he said gently, 'don't turn me away.' His hands were caressing her slim flanks, moving up the bare skin of her back to touch the thick tumble of her hair. 'You're a very special woman, my love.' His voice was rough, but quiet. 'I just know we've met before. But if it wasn't in this lifetime, then it must have been in some other one, because I feel that I'm acquainted with you. The important thing is that we don't lose one another again.'

'Hmm,' Sophie said, keeping her casual smile with an effort, 'the cognac is making you unwise, Mr Hart. That kind of talk is for shallow people—not persons of deep feeling, like you and I.'

'I mean it,' he said, his eyes tightening. 'I know we've barely met each other, but there's something about you that...' He didn't finish the sentence. 'You must feel that, too. I know you do.'

'I feel that it's past my bedtime,' she said, trying to sound relaxed. 'So if you'll let me go——'

'Damn you!' he whispered. 'How can you be so cool when I'm burning?'

Then, with smooth power, he had lifted her off her feet, into his arms. She gasped in shock, clinging to his neck, her long legs dangling.

'Kyle!'

He carried her into the bedroom, and laid her down against the white coverlet, sitting beside her and trapping her by leaning over her on one arm. He smiled down at her as she lay helpless, her breasts rising and falling as she panted slightly. 'Now I've got you where I want you.'

'This is the basest kind of treachery,' she protested. 'Let me up!'

'In a moment.' He bent to kiss her neck, his breath warm against her fine skin. Sophie tried to turn away, but he had put her in a helpless position. His mouth moved across her throat, finding the soft hollow at its base, his lips warm and hungry. She gasped involuntarily as his warm breath brushed the sensitive shell of her ear.

'Kyle, you promised! Please, let me go——'

His kiss stopped her words, his warm mouth dominating her without effort. An electric thrill rolled down her stomach as she felt his tongue, smooth and moist, probe between her lips.

She arched against him, fear and desire struggling in her. He was caressing her body with rough tenderness, brushing the curve of her breasts, the swell of her hips underneath the black silk.

'Let's take your mask off, just for once,' he said huskily. 'Let's see who you really are.'

'Kyle, *no*!' she protested, as he started easing the material away from her breasts.

'I want you so much.' His deep voice was almost a whisper, and she sensed, rather than heard, the tremor that underlay it. He stared down into the wide grey depths of her eyes. His face was half in shadow, all his male desire concentrated in the tawny eyes that devoured her.

He was so strong; she tried to stop him from pulling the strapless top down, but she could not. In the soft light, her skin was the colour of burned honey, her breasts creamy-pale, demarcated by the line of her costume.

'I'm glad you don't suntan topless,' Kyle said quietly. 'You're so demure, so cool and maidenly. It's driven me mad, right from the start...' He leaned forward to kiss the valley between her breasts, inhaling the scent of her flesh. 'And you smell so sweet.' He spoke with his mouth close against her skin. 'That perfume has been haunting me all night. It's like you, it tantalises me. I feel I know it, and yet it's so new and strange to me...'

It was so hard to control her reactions; a kind of electricity was flowing from him into her veins, charging her with his desire, until she felt as though every nerve were stretched tight. His mouth roamed over her breasts, his kisses warm and tender against the soft flesh, the delicate arch of her collarbone, the aching stars of her nipples.

Sophie's body was moving with a will of its own, a primitive hunger that paid no heed to her reason. She was arching to him, her fingers roaming through the crisp hair that clung and twined round them, as though it had an amorous life of its own.

Her mouth was forming his name, her panting breath making the words ragged and uneven. Her mind was screaming commands at her, to get out, get away, run home as fast as her legs would carry her.

But what had she worn this dress for, what had she made herself beautiful for—what did she exist for—if not for this?

Sophie drew him close, as if it were suddenly she who was the demanding one, and he the pursued. His body was so hard and strong, its potency overwhelming her senses. She had longed to touch him for so long that her caress was almost rough in its explosive release.

She gasped out loud as his mouth tasted the tender pink tips of her breasts, the caress of his tongue a passionate adoration. Sophie could feel them tighten with desire in his mouth, hardly aware that she was digging her nails into the hard muscles of his back, as though urging him to unleash the cruelty she had always suspected was in him.

His teeth closed gently around the taut buds, the sensation at first shockingly intense, then changing to a languorous heat that invaded her thighs, her womb, the centre of her need.

At last, he drew away from her, and rolled on to his back, pulling her on top of him. The face that looked up at her was magnificent, passion making it more beautiful than she had ever seen it before. The curving male mouth was imperious.

'Take my shirt off.'

Why could she not disobey the whispered command? Her shaking fingers were fumbling with the buttons, her hair tumbling about her face as she pressed tiny, shy kisses on each inch of velvety bronze skin that was revealed. He smelled so good, warm and male and clean, and she thrilled to the way his breathing grew harsh and fast at her clumsy, timid caresses.

The night was like silk, cool and silent, wrapping them in dark arms. The world outside was ceasing to exist, their bodies becoming the only universe that mattered.

Tender with passionate hunger, Sophie tasted the dark
skin of his belly, feeling the curling black hair brush her
lips as her tongue drew moistly towards the dark core
of his navel. He groaned, his arms reaching for her.

'I want you, Sophie,' he said, almost fiercely. 'I've
never wanted anyone the way I want you.'

She sank her cheek against his bare skin, closing her
eyes. Her arm touched his loins unwittingly, brushing
the hard, swollen arousal there; Kyle's half-stifled gasp
of reaction made a wave of dizziness wash through her
mind. He lifted himself on one arm, staring into Sophie's
dark bewildered eyes with ruthless intensity.

'The moment I set eyes on you, this was already happening in my mind. I've made love to you a dozen, a
hundred times already.' He smiled briefly, tawny eyes
seeming to speak to her very soul. 'Sometimes it was
slow and unbearably drawn-out. Sometimes it was swift
and savage. But I never dreamed, not once, that it could
be as beautiful as this.'

'Oh, Kyle,' Sophie whispered, helpless in the force of
her feelings for him.

'Let's not hurry,' he murmured, his mouth seeking
hers. 'We've got all night...'

He cupped her breasts as he kissed her, his thumbs
moving with slow appreciation across her sensitised aur-
eoles. She was lost, her mind flooded with patterns of
colour, like the bright depths of a kaleidoscope, ever
changing, never escaping the brilliant circle of desire.

Her own hand had come to rest at the base of his
belly, sensing the heat of his manhood through the thin
material. The way he moved begged her to move her
hand lower, and her fingertips moved like shy butterflies
to obey, tracing the shrouded mystery of his desire so
gently that it was almost impossible he could feel it; and
yet he moaned, deep in his throat, as though her tim-
orous touch had been the most expert of caresses.

Her heart was pounding, her mind spinning on waves of dizzy heat as she stroked him there, feeling his possessive touch at her breasts.

Had she meant this to happen? Was this part of her so-called plan, that she should wind up making love to Kyle Hart on the eve of her departure?

He was kissing her mouth as he caressed her naked back, her flanks, her hips, the slit in her sarong now proving a fatal breach in her defences as he slid his hand along the inside of her thigh, her position offering no resistance to the questing fingers that moved expertly towards the wisp of lace that was all that protected her virginity.

Sophie had never gone this far with any man before. These were regions where she had never trodden, feelings she had never dreamed of. But then, she had never been with a man like Kyle before.. The compelling sexuality of this man had overwhelmed her from the start. But she had never stopped wanting him.

She, too, had done this a hundred times in her imagination already. But she had not possessed the honesty, or the self-knowledge, to admit it.

Her thoughts broke up in a silent explosion of colour as she felt Kyle's fingers reach the moist, silken skin of her loins, touching the melting substance of her womanhood, finding the soaring apex of her desire with a caress that brought both gasping release and a completely new surge of hunger.

The time for reserve was over. Suddenly, their bodies were pressed together, their mouths kissing with a feverish intensity as their hands caressed, tormented, excited one another beyond endurance.

There was no more doubt, no more thought of the consequences of the morrow, or the morality of what she was doing, in Sophie's mind. Her mind was his, both of them focused on the ever more urgent necessity of union, of knowing each other well enough for the act of love.

An eternity later, they both paused, staring at one another in tense wonder as they lay on the white bed-cover. He was naked to the waist, his body dark and formidably male in the soft light. She, with her chestnut hair tumbled round her flushed cheeks, and her black dress rumpled about her slender waist, made a picture of wanton eroticism.

'Kyle,' she said tightly, her voice feeling as though she hadn't used it for months, 'there's something you don't know.'

For a moment, amusement took the place of desire in his eyes. White teeth glinted between tanned lips as he laughed softly. 'Is there, little cool Sophie? And what might that be?'

Her mouth opened, but no words were formed. She could not go on without telling him. And yet, if she told him now—if she told him, and he was angry, or laughed...

Unlike last year in Brighton, Kyle's attraction towards her in Jamaica had been swift and warm. As she'd seen the interest in her awaken in his eyes, so she'd started to dread discovery. It had stopped being a game, long ago. If he once remembered her as Maisie Wilkin, that ugly, drab creature he'd once found so repulsive, would all his interest in her not swiftly evaporate, and vanish forever?

She flinched suddenly, as though a rough blow had landed across her mouth.

At first, all she'd wanted was to have a bit of mischievous fun with him. At least, that was what she'd told herself. She'd had something in mind when her little game with Kyle had started, but the logic of it had somehow got distorted, broken up like a reflection in troubled waters.

And now she was deathly afraid. She had been afraid from the very start. Afraid that, once again, her feelings were going to be trampled on.

She'd faced this moment from the very beginning, when she had first set eyes on him down at the beach. And she had already weighed up the prospects, and had come down on the side of three weeks of certain heaven, rather than risk the chance of nothing at all.

But had she made the right choice?

She'd never known such perfection as these three weeks. And tonight, as he'd held her in his arms, she had felt that Kyle's feelings were real, and that they had been on the brink of an experience that had depth and beauty in full measure.

But it had all been false, it was all tottering on the edge of a horrible disaster, because of what she knew and he didn't.

'What is it?' he asked in concern, seeing the colour drain from her glowing face. 'Sophie?' Kyle drew her close, his mouth seeking hers for the gentlest of caresses. 'What is it, my darling? You look as though you've seen a ghost.'

'I have,' she whispered.

'What is it that I'm supposed to know? Tell me.'

'Oh, Kyle,' she whimpered. 'If you only knew how I've prayed that you wouldn't do this to me...'

'Don't you want me to make love to you?'

'Oh, yes...but you don't understand. And when you do understand, I'm so afraid of what you'll feel...'

He stared at her, eyes dark and puzzled as he tried to fathom what she was saying.

And in the taut silence came the faint, muffled crying of a child from the next room, desolate and afraid.

'Emma,' he said quietly. 'She has nightmares. The baby-sitter will put her back to sleep.'

But the crying only increased in volume and intensity. 'You must go to her,' Sophie said, releasing him with a deathly ache in her heart. 'She needs someone she knows.'

His fingers bit into her wrists like manacles.

'God, I'm suddenly so afraid you won't be here when I get back,' he said tautly.

'I will be,' she promised, feeling a thick lump in her throat.

Kyle stared into her eyes for a tense moment longer. Then he rose fluidly to his feet, and pulled his silk dressing-gown off the chair.

He left without a word, closing the door behind him.

Sophie, too, got unsteadily to her feet. Her breasts and loins were aching with unfulfilled desire. She caught sight of herself in the mirror, the intense eroticism of her own appearance shocking her raw sensibilities.

Clumsily, she hooked the dress back over her naked breasts, trying to restore some order to her dishevelled clothing. It was not going to happen tonight. In a moment she was going to go back to her room, and tomorrow she was going back to England. Her eyes were blurred with unshed tears as she groped for Kyle's hairbrush, and started blindly brushing her hair.

She listened to the distant sound of Emma's crying, hearing it fade away into silence.

She had reached a point in her relationship with Kyle beyond which she could not go.

She couldn't let him make love to her, not without telling him who she really was.

And she couldn't face what his reaction might be to that disclosure. Not now, not tonight.

The door opened, and Kyle came back into the room, his eyes darkening as they saw her dressed.

'Sophie...*damn*! I knew that would be the end of it.'

'Tomorrow is another day,' she said, taking a deep breath of the cool night air in an effort to steady the surging in her veins.

'Do I have to take that as a dismissal?' Kyle asked, coming to take her in his arms.

Sophie's mouth drew into an unsteady smile. 'Tomorrow is another day,' she repeated.

'Then what are you crying about?' he replied, kissing her temples gently. 'What did you want to tell me that was so important?'

She looked at him from under thick lashes that were wet with tears. Tomorrow was going to be a very different awakening from the one he expected. 'Nothing. I'm just not . . . not very experienced at all this.'

Kyle looked down at her with an expression in his green eyes that made her heart turn over inside her.

'Are you telling me that you're a virgin?' he asked quietly.

She hesitated, then nodded with a laugh that was midway to a sob. 'Yes. Partly that, yes.'

'And you want more time to think about it?' he said, even more gently.

She nodded, her throat too choked for speech.

Kyle smiled slightly, but not mockingly. 'Don't think about it for too long. I might just get ill with wanting you in the meantime.'

Again, that half-laugh, half-sob rose in her throat. 'Thank you for a lovely evening. All of it. It's been like nothing I've ever known before.'

'If I said the same thing, you probably wouldn't believe me. But it's true.' He kissed her vulnerable, slightly swollen lips softly, cupping her oval face in his hands. 'Do you really want to go?' he whispered huskily.

She nodded, and he walked her to her own room. Outside her door he reached for her again, but Sophie gave him a warning glance.

'I think you've kissed me quite enough for one night,' she pleaded. 'I don't think I could take much more.'

'If I get any sleep,' he promised, 'I'm going to dream of number one hundred and one.'

She smiled up at him, her eyes lingering on one of the most magnificent male faces she would ever see. Then she held out the gardenia he had given her. 'I've loved tonight. All of it. Until tomorrow.'

He took the flower. 'Until tomorrow.'

She let herself into her room, and locked the door.

Her eyes were blurred with tears again, tears that now spilled hotly down her cheeks, unchecked. She fought her emotions down fiercely. There wasn't time for absurd sentimental indulgences. She brushed her wet cheeks, and checked her watch. Almost five. Already, the sky was lightening outside, and she caught the smoky morning smell of a distant fire. In two hours' time, she would have to be ready to leave.

It wasn't worth taking off her make-up, but she stripped off the sarong dress. The tips of her breasts were still painful with eager desire, her loins liquid and throbbing, but she fought that feeling down, too. She packed the dress, and the last of her belongings, and started getting ready for her departure.

The only things she didn't pack were her pyjamas, which she put on, her sponge-bag, and a light dress to wear on the flight.

There was only one way for her to know how seriously Kyle Hart felt about her, and that was to do what she had originally planned to do: go back to England, leaving him a letter telling him who she really was.

She sat at the desk, and pulled a sheet of hotel writing-paper towards her. There were no more tears in her eyes as she started to write.

> Dear Kyle,
> Once upon a time there was a girl who went for a walk on Brighton sands, and overhead a man talking about her to her friend. What she heard him say about her was painful. It wounded her vanity, and made her wish, for a while, that she were someone else.
> By the time you read this, I'll be on my way home. I'm sorry to have perpetrated a deception on you. You were right all along, of course. You and I have met before, but it was not an occasion which I remember with any pleasure, and so I took care not to remind you of it. Now I wish I had done

so, at the start. But it's too late for wishes.

If your memory needs further prompting, you can see me as I was on BBC 2 at eight p.m. on Thursday the 15th August. I've changed since then, but I was the absurd one, with those awful clothes and glasses.

I can only hope that you'll understand why I deceived you, and how much it has cost me.

Sophie hesitated for a long while, staring at the paper with absent eyes. Should she add something like, 'Please get in touch with me again?' She could just add her London phone number, or even her address. But her pen hesitated over the paper.

If he wanted to find her again, he could locate her easily enough. Hélène, for one, could tell him where she lived. And if he didn't want to find her...

Well, there was nothing she could do about that. She would have to leave it up to him. She had no other choice.

If he really cared about her, he would come to her again, and they could start their relationship on a fresh footing. If he felt only disgust at the revelation, or if his feelings had never been serious to start with, then she would never see him again. It was as simple as that.

There seemed nothing more she could say. After a moment, she signed the note, 'Maisie'. As an afterthought, she took the Giorgio Armani bottle out of her bag and let one small drop fall on the paper.

She read the note. It would sting, and at first it would seem to have hit too hard, and too far below the belt. But what else could she do?

She folded the note, sealed it, and wrote Kyle's name and room number on the envelope. She propped it up on her desk, ready to give to reception later, as she left.

Then she climbed into bed, and curled up under the sheet. She pushed sorrow firmly away from her mind.

There would be time enough later to think about what she had done, and grieve for what might have been.

Now she closed her eyes, and let memories of the brightest night of her life take her down the tunnel of sleep.

CHAPTER FIVE

WHAT had been the point of it all?

As the Jumbo descended through layers of misty cloud towards Heathrow, at twenty minutes to midnight, Sophie was thinking about what had happened over the past three weeks.

She'd once adored Kyle Hart. Meeting him again hadn't exactly quenched the glowing embers of that feeling. In fact, being in his company for three blissful weeks had been more like a gale, fanning the glow into a full-scale forest fire.

Why hadn't she told him who she really was right at the start? Why hadn't she just given their relationship a chance to recover from what had happened in Brighton last year, and let the Caribbean sunshine ease away all pain, all anger, so that they could make a new start?

It was too late for such reproaches. His awakening this morning would have put a cold end to any such dreams.

She thought of him reading her note, thought of his expression, the way his face would have changed. She'd once thought of that moment with relish. Not any more. If that was a triumph, then it was a mean one, and one she hadn't even stayed to witness.

What kind of brainstorm had she been through? Looking back, she must have been insane to have played that kind of trick on a man like Kyle.

Now, approaching a rainy London, she was wondering who had really been punished, and who had really been hurt.

'Ladies and gentlemen, this is your stewardess speaking. Please fasten your seat-belts and extinguish your cigarettes. Passengers are requested to make sure their seats are in the upright position for landing, and to refrain from smoking until they are in the terminal building.'

Sophie reached absently for her seat-belt.

A song was running through her head, the bitter-sweet refrain of 'Jamaica Farewell': 'My heart is down, my head is turnin' around, I had to leave a little girl in Kingston town...'

But she knew that Kyle wasn't the forever kind. Had she let herself be drawn into the maelstrom of an affair with him, blown on the wings of a Caribbean hurricane from Ocho Rios to the Cayman Islands, she would almost certainly have ended up with a broken heart and broken dreams.

So maybe getting away from Kyle, and leaving him with that slap in the face, had been the best thing she could have done.

But no amount of rationalising could take the ache away from her heart, or the depression from her mind. All she knew was that she was a day away, a lifetime away, from the only man who had ever really touched her heart.

The landing was bumpy, and the tarmac was wet with drizzle. The ground staff seemed to look at the incoming passengers with world-weary, cynical eyes. The familiar smells of Heathrow hit Sophie with a wave of melancholy. Fighting through the crowds of people, she decided to take a taxi home rather than battle with her heavy suitcases in the Underground late at night. She didn't want to come down to earth with too much of a bump just yet.

Two and a half hours later, she was falling into bed in her tiny flat in St John's Wood.

It was on a main road, and after the peace of Jamaica the noise of the traffic outside when she woke next morning was intrusive. Despite Mrs Flanagan's languid efforts, the pokiness of the place was something of a blow after the airy room at the San Antonio, and when

she remembered the rent she was paying for it distaste
for her surroundings settled like a cloud over her head.
Would she ever make enough money at her job to afford
a better place? London was so hideously expensive these
days, yet no one with aspirations to a career in acting
could afford not to live here.

The black silk sarong was the first thing she found
when she opened her big suitcase. She lifted the dress
out, and stared at it, grey eyes sombre. The faint smell
of the Giorgio Armani perfume was still on it, reminding her poignantly of her last night in Jamaica.

The night before last? It all seemed to have happened
an eternity ago. His kisses, his touch. The way he'd asked
her to sail away into the mists of romance with him...

Would he ever get back in touch with her?

She was starting to have a terrible feeling that she
would never hear from Kyle Hart again.

Why should he bother to get back in touch with her,
anyway? She'd left no invitation for him to do so. In
fact, that note might be construed as deliberately final.
She thought back, biting her full lower lip, and wished
she could remember exactly what she'd said. Five o'clock
in the morning, under the influence of Jamaican rum
and Kyle's kisses, had not been exactly the best time for
balanced literary composition.

Had she made it more harsh than she'd wanted to?

Had she really envisaged her return here as being like
this, with no possibility of ever seeing Kyle again?

Suddenly, she dropped the black dress and ran to the
telephone. She had the San Antonio's number in her
diary, and she hunted frantically through the telephone
book to find the STD code for Jamaica.

She dialled the number, and sat tensely by the telephone. It would be eight o'clock in Jamaica right now.
She would start off by apologising for that ridiculous
note. Or *trying* to apologise. God, he must be feeling so
awful by now. She just hoped he would listen to her.
Then she would tell him exactly how she felt about him,

how much he meant to her. Then she would ask him
to——

'San Antonio Hotel, can I help you?'

'Hello! This is Sophie Aspen, calling from England.
I've been staying in room 315 for the past three
weeks——'

'Yes, Miss Aspen,' the receptionist said brightly. 'Have
you left any personal property behind? Anything we can
do?'

'No, I haven't left anything. I'd like to speak to Mr
Kyle Hart, if I might.'

'Oh, Miss Aspen, you've missed Mr Hart.'

'Has he gone somewhere?'

'He checked out yesterday,' the receptionist replied.

'Checked out?' she gasped. 'Where has he gone to?'

'I have no idea, I'm afraid. He informed Reception
he was leaving right after breakfast, and that's what he
did. I could take a message, in case he gets back in touch
with us, but he didn't say he was going to.'

'If he *does* get in touch,' Sophie said tautly, 'will you
ask him to telephone me, please?'

She left her number, and went back to her unpacking
with a dark sense of acute frustration. Where had he
gone to? What did his suddenly checking out like that
mean? She worried miserably for half an hour. Then
reaction set in to her mood of loss. Damn it, girl! She
made herself a cup of coffee, cursing herself. Forget him,
for God's sake. He's a shallow, heartless, careless man,
to whom you mean no more than a snap of his fingers.
Forget him. You've got him out of your system at last;
be content with that. He was never the man for you.
Don't let your head be turned a second time!

Forcing herself to face hard practicality, she set about
finishing off the cleaning job Mrs Flanagan had started.

There were two telephone calls that evening.

The first, which arrived midway during her dinner of
salad and cheese, had her scrambling for the phone, her
heart pounding in the expectation that it would be from

Kyle. It wasn't. It was from her mother in Scarborough, to check that she'd arrived safely back.

'You don't sound very cheerful, darling,' she commented, after listening to Sophie's rather lacklustre assurances that the holiday had been enjoyable. 'Maybe you should have had someone to keep you company, after all.'

'To tell the truth,' Sophie admitted, 'I'm just not feeling all that jolly.'

'Disappointed it's all over?'

'In a way. And I think I might be getting one of those summer colds...'

'Poor thing! Get an early night. We're all so excited about the film. I just wish you were able to come home to watch it with us.'

'So do I,' Sophie sighed. 'But I just can't. I'm scheduled to be working on the commercial that day, and the next.'

'Our baby, on television,' her mother marvelled. 'I still can't get over it.'

'You'll get a shock when you see me in *The Elmtree Road Murders*,' she warned. Her family hadn't seen her while she'd been playing Maisie, and didn't know what to expect. 'Just remember that I'm not in a very flattering role.'

'We're expecting the worst,' came the laughing reply. 'As long as we can recognise you. Darling, your cousin wants to come down and stay with you.'

'Jenny?'

'Yes. She'll be on holiday from next week, and you know how she loves London.'

'I do,' Sophie said, a shade wryly. That was all she needed right now. She really wasn't in the mood to have her vivacious and rather spoilt younger cousin to stay. Jenny on holiday was, at best, something of a handful, and previous visits had left Sophie exhausted. But blood was thicker than water.

'If you're too busy to have her——' her mother began.

'No, no. I'll be working during the day from the thirteenth to the sixteenth, but apart from that I'll be free. Tell her I'd love to have her.'

'Are you sure?'

'Yes, of course! Tell her to come down as soon as she can.'

'She'll be thrilled. You get yourself into bed now, and take an aspirin. My bet is you'll be right as rain tomorrow. Goodbye, darling.'

''Bye, Mum.'

By the time the second call came at nine, she was less sanguine in her hopes. It wasn't from Kyle, either, but from Joey Gilmour, Sophie's agent.

'Welcome back to civilisation,' he boomed. 'I nearly rang you in Ocho Rios!'

'Why, what's the news?'

'Only two separate and distinct movie directors anxious to secure your services, that's all.'

'Joey!'

'Well, don't get too excited. Neither of them's Steven Spielberg. But apparently word's getting round about the great performance you put in for *The Elmtree Road Murders*. The people who've seen the edited tapes say you're sensational. I knew you would be. Come round to my office tomorrow at ten, and I'll tell you all about it.'

'Oh, please tell me about it *now*,' she begged, sitting down by the phone with bright eyes. 'Who are they? What are the films?'

'The directors are John Payne and Franco Luciani.'

'Never heard of them,' Sophie said, slightly disappointed.

'They're both young and relatively unknown,' Joey replied, 'except in arty circles. However, they've turned in good work recently. I've seen both scripts, and they aren't bad.'

'And the roles?'

'In John Payne's script you'd be playing a psycho-path. You go around posing as a nurse, and murdering your patients.'

'Ugh! And in the other?'

'The other role's a young drug addict, called Marjorie. You die tragically just as you discover love. It'll be filmed in Italy, in Pisa. That's where Franco Luciani comes from.'

'What language is the script in?'

'English. The exciting thing is that this is a lead role.'

'Wow,' she laughed. 'I can't believe it. I've never even met this man, and he wants me to play the lead in his next film?'

'He's very keen about you, and apparently his backers agree. He's had access to some of the *Elmtree Road* tapes, and he's very impressed. Quote: "If she can do that, she can do anything," unquote!'

'Gosh! I don't know what to say.'

'There are various problems,' Joey cautioned. 'For one thing, he's working on a very small budget. I've checked out his backers, and they haven't given him much leeway. His last film was praised to the skies by the critics, but it didn't make a penny at the box-office, so this is something of a shoestring operation. That means that he's not in a position to pay anything like the fee you got for *Elmtree Road*. On the other hand, nor is John Payne. Frankly, if we wait around, we'll probably get better offers. But I'll give you the scripts next week, Sophie. I've got them down here in my office. You can have a think about them both.'

'OK.'

'So how was Jamaica?'

'Oh, it was beautiful. I had a lovely time.'

'You can show me your holiday snaps next week. And I'll fill you in on all the gossip since you've been away. You must be worn out. Sleep well, Sarah Bernhardt!'

*   *   *

Kyle didn't get in touch that night, nor through the week that followed. She rang the San Antonio, just to be sure, but he hadn't been back in touch with the hotel. They had no idea where he might be.

She went to see Joey Gilmour, to pick up the scripts and discuss her prospects.

'There's no rush to accept either part,' Joey counselled. 'If we wait a month or two, you might get an offer of a part you like better. In fact, you might get a whole lot of offers!'

'That seems a little callous——'

'It's a hard world, Sophie! Frankly, I think these two young guys have both had the same idea—to get in before you become hot property, which may just happen after *The Elmtree Road Murders* is screened next month. They're both working on very limited budgets, and they aren't exactly offering top dollar, either of them. They want a talented actress at a cheap fee, and that isn't so easy these days.'

'Am I really a talented actress?'

'You tell me,' Joey smiled. 'I think you're very talented. You'd be making much less than you did for the BBC, and working for a longer period. On the other hand, it wouldn't hurt your reputation to work for either of these two guys. They have something of a cult following in intellectual circles, and they could be the Fellinis or the Viscontis of the future.'

'Can we afford to put them off? Two job offers is two more than I've ever had, even to play a drug addict and a psychopath!'

'Yes,' Joey said, more soberly. 'That's something else. I know you're afraid of being typecast, after Maisie. We don't want you to be playing oddball parts for the rest of your career. So we'll have to think about this situation in role terms, as well.'

'Oh,' she replied. 'I'm delighted about this, Joey, don't get me wrong. But you're right. I do want to pick my next part carefully.'

'Of course you do. And I'm here to help. You go and read those scripts, and have a think. Remember, I can only give advice. The final decision is down to you.'

Sophie started reading the scripts that afternoon, and tried to think logically about the future. But really, she was concerned with little else but Kyle, wondering what he was doing, whether he had taken that tour of the Caribbean with Emma after all, whether he had returned from Jamaica yet, whether he would forgive her for her deception. Wondering whether he would ring.

The only answer to those questions was the silence that deepened, day by day, as the weekend approached.

By the following Sunday, there had still been no phone call, no visit, no letter. Nothing. The days passed, and with each one, a little something died inside Sophie.

Seldom had time passed in such depression for her.

And she had plenty of time to fill in before she started work on the commercial. She had her hair cut and styled, after agreeing with the art director of the advertising agency, into a fairly short modern style that showed off her slender neck, but left plenty of glossy chestnut curls to frame her face.

She also, at the same art director's instigation, paid two visits to beauty clinics for a facial and to get her eyebrows shaped.

She re-read both scripts carefully. John Payne's script, about the psychopathic nurse, was violent and bloody, and didn't ring any bells with her at all. But the other one did.

Franco Luciani, whoever he was, had written his own sensitive and very touching script, based on a recent novel called *The First Day of Autumn*. The film was to have the same title. The more Sophie read the script, the more impressed she was. It was a simple story: a young English girl who can't shake her addiction to heroin goes to Italy, meets and falls in love with a good-looking Italian boy who tries to save her, but dies in the end, leaving him heartbroken. The central role of Marjorie, the young drug-addict, was a good one, anyone with any feel for drama could see that at a glance, and the script as a whole had the feel of a prospect that would succeed. It was a contemporary love story. It was moving, it was glamorous, and it was exciting.

In short, Sophie had the feeling that it was a winner. Discussions with Joey confirmed that he was not so sanguine, believing that she could get far more money if she waited. But he had another bit of news about the film.

'The male lead is going to be Luigi Canotta.'

'Wow,' Sophie said appreciatively. Though Canotta was not all that well known in England, he was very much a rising star in Italy. He was also a strikingly handsome man, and something of a younger generation sex symbol.

'Yeah,' Joey grinned, watching her expression. 'Very good-looking, and quite a man. You'd be in good company, at any rate.'

However, they confirmed their decision to hold off giving any reply, or even meeting the director, until *The Elmtree Road Murders* was screened.

'I'll stall him for another couple of weeks,' Joey said, 'and see what turns up. In the meantime, I've told him you're reading the script and thinking about it.'

The weekend dragged by in an infinity of loneliness and nostalgia. She was haunted by thoughts of Kyle.

Thoughts of his kindness and humour, the fun they'd shared.

Thoughts of his incredible physical appeal for her. That was the hardest thing to forget. Images of his beauty had been stamped into her mind forever, memories of that tanned, muscled body, and the way it had loved her.

She lay in bed, suffocating and restless with the burning heat of the passion he'd awoken in her, remembering the dizzy intimacy of their caresses until she thought she would go mad with frustrated desire.

There was no release, only an increasing imprisonment with her own hunger for Kyle. Where was he? Why didn't he call or write, if only to abuse her with angry names?

Jenny arrived to stay on Monday, looking prettier than ever, announcing that she would stay for four or five weeks.

'Is that too long?' she asked, innocent blue eyes wide.

'Of course not,' Sophie smiled. 'We never see each other these days. How're things at university?'

'Marvellous. I'm having this *wild* affair with one of the lecturers,' she confided gaily to a shocked Sophie. 'Oh, don't look like that! He's practically old enough to be my father.'

'And that makes it better?'

'At least he isn't in the maths department,' she said with a giggle. 'Anyway, I prefer older men—that way it can't ever get very serious, can it?' Jenny said practically, and plunged into the steamy details of her love-life.

Sophie, acutely conscious of her own inexperience, listened in alternating amusement and horror. How had Jenny grown into such an uninhibited womanhood, while she herself, two years older, was still a virgin? How did Jenny always manage to be the one in control of her relationships with men, while Sophie's only real love-affair with a man had just ended in disaster?

From the day of her arrival, the telephone glowed red-hot from Jenny's breathy, interminable phone calls to men, and not just to the love-lorn lecturer in York, either—there seemed to be at least four on the go.

Despite their differences of temperament, they had always been good friends. And the presence of her unashamedly frivolous, flirtatious cousin for company was a distraction, in some measure, from her inner ache about Kyle.

Jenny got her out of the flat, too. They went to all the latest shows, Sophie getting tickets through friends in the profession, met a lot of acquaintances, and went to their fair share of parties—all of which gave Jenny the idea that being an out-of-work actress was a better deal than being employed in any other profession.

On the thirteenth, two days before the screening of *The Elmtree Road Murders*, Sophie stopped being an out-of-work actress, and started filming for the television commercial. It was scarcely demanding work: her part consisted of sitting practically naked in a bathtub of foamy water, lathering various parts of her body, with a dreamy expression on her face.

Jenny, whom she wangled on to the set to watch the performance, was amused.

'You're going to have the cleanest right arm in London,' she announced after the seventeenth retake of Sophie soaping her arm. 'Darling, I'm sure *I* could do that just as well as you!'

Sophie, shivering slightly in her bathrobe, shrugged. 'I'm sure you could.'

'Why do they keep doing the same bit over and over again?'

'Advertising work is so meticulous. They get less than a minute to put their message over—a very expensive minute. So every second has to be perfect. But it can be rather dull.'

'Well, I'm bored stiff!' There was a glint in Jenny's blue eyes. 'There's a rather gorgeous boy over there. Think I'll just go and ask him for a light.'

'What happened to your lighter?' Sophie asked in all innocence.

'It's just stopped working,' Jenny smirked, taking out a Dunhill and slipping off towards the technician in question.

'Sophie!' the director carolled. 'Ready for a retake?'

With a grimace at her cousin's elegant back, Sophie rose to get back into action, this time soaping her throat and shoulders.

'In this sequence we want to emphasise the *tactile* and *fragrant* qualities of the product,' he urged, helping her into the lukewarm tub under the baking spotlights. 'It has to feel slippery, slick, soapy. You absolutely *love* smoothing it over your throat. And then the perfume hits you, and you inhale deeply, *rapturously*...'

Jenny's uninhibited presence distracted Sophie a little from her brooding over Kyle. Her dreams, however, were full of him these days. He came to her almost as soon as her eyes closed, warm and real in memories of Caribbean sunshine, his magnificent body naked and eager for her, his lovemaking overwhelming her like the deep blue sea...

Sophie was thinking of him when she sat curled up on the sofa next to Jenny, with her heart in her throat as the announcer introduced *The Elmtree Road Murders*. She was hugging her stomach, which was aching with nerves.

'What are you so jittery about?' Jenny laughed. 'It's all over and done with now. There's nothing you can do about anything any more.'

'I know. But I'm as tense as though I were going out to do it live at the Palladium!'

'How many people are watching this?'

'They predicted around seven million.'

'Seven million...?' Her cousin shook her head. 'That's a lot of people! I'm going to tell everyone at university that you're my cousin!'

They both stared at the screen as the film began.

It was obvious at once that the production department had done a superb job. *The Elmtree Road Murders* exuded quality right away, from the moody theme music to the 1920s-style graphics of the credits.

The opening scenes, shot in the Brighton boarding-house, had a brooding, atmospheric quality. Hélène le

Bon was on screen with one of the male leads. Coming over very cool and graceful, she radiated professionalism to Sophie's eye.

'Doesn't she look elegant?' Jenny said. Her blue eyes were bright and wide, her golden-red hair glinted in the light. 'She's such a beautiful actress. When do you come on?'

'In the next scene.'

It was all coming back as she watched, the atmosphere of those summery days in Brighton. The happiness, the pain. She would always feel ambivalent about this film; so much had happened to her during it, and after it, to make her emotional. But looking at the finished product now, she felt a thrill of pleasure at having been associated with such a quality production.

She wondered with a sudden stab of pain whether Kyle was one of those seven million, watching the screen now, somewhere in London.

'Sophie!'

Jenny's scream of laughter snapped her out of her reverie. She looked up, and saw herself. There she was, on the screen. Or rather, there was Maisie.

'Is that really you?' Jenny demanded, hands trying to stifle her laughter. 'I can scarcely recognise you! God, I had no *idea* you'd had to put on so much weight. And that awful hair—they've turned you into a fright!'

'Yes, I do look rather depressing, don't I?'

Sophie tried not to wince at Jenny's laughter. Indeed, the black-haired, rotund figure bore hardly any resemblance to Sophie Aspen as she now was. Everything was different, even the movements, the expression on the sallow features, the voice. The glowering housemaid radiated an air of hostility and resentment as a brick wall radiated heat at the end of a summer's day.

'I'm not so sure about telling people we're related any more! No wonder you were embarrassed about yourself,' Jenny gurgled. 'I wouldn't have let anyone make me look as awful as that for a thousand pounds!'

The mixture of feelings inside Sophie was almost too complicated to make sense. She tried to be detached, professional, noting the way the scenes had been cut and edited, trying to pick faults in her own acting.

But inwardly, a dull, throbbing pain in her heart reminded her of Kyle. Of the way he would have seen her during that week in Brighton.

She had been so unattractive. That was her overwhelming thought. No wonder he'd laughed at her. No wonder he'd found her adoration of him absurd!

'Anyway,' Jenny grinned, turning to her cousin, 'you're not a bad actress, despite that hair. In fact, you're rather good!'

Sophie smiled wryly, watching herself playing Maisie Wilkin. The intensity of her own performance was impressive, she had to admit that. The little figures on the screen moved and spoke, strutted and fretted. The story unfolded. But Sophie wasn't involved with the plot any more.

Three weeks. Three weeks without a word from him. If he'd had the slightest intention of seeing her again, he would have been in touch by now.

Damn that letter; *damn* her stupid pride!

If she'd told him who she was, that last night in Jamaica, she might be watching this in his arms now.

What could his mood be towards her? Anger? Indifference?

The latter, most likely. If he'd felt a momentary pique at the one that got away, Kyle Hart was the sort of man who would have no trouble finding himself a consolation prize. In fact, he would probably have done so instantly, just to prove to himself that he could do it . . .

Sophie's eyes blurred with tears, the screen becoming merely a dancing square of light. She turned her head aside so that Jenny wouldn't notice. She was experiencing the horrible feeling that she had lost the only man she had ever really cared about.

*   *   *

The telephone started ringing before the final credits had finished rolling.

First through were her parents, her mother weepy, even her tough old father husky with emotion. 'You were super, Sophie, just great,' he said. 'You have a real talent, my girl. We're all so proud of you.'

'Weren't you a little shocked to see the part I was in?' she asked.

'Shocked? Of course not. You're an actress. And we know what you look like in real life!'

More professional, but no less enthusiastic praise came from Eleanor Bragg, Sophie's tutor at drama school, who rang immediately afterwards.

'That was a fine performance for someone as young as you,' she told Sophie. 'I can't think of many young actresses who could have held their own so well, playing against a performer of the calibre of Hélène le Bon. As for those courtroom scenes... I'm very proud of you, Sophie.'

Jenny cracked the bottle of supermarket champagne that had been chilling in the fridge all day, but they didn't get much chance to drink it. The telephone kept ringing every few minutes. Several friends and colleagues rang in quick succession, some of them people she hadn't heard from in months, and later on Joey Gilmour got through, characteristically outdoing everyone else.

'You were bloody fantastic,' he boomed down the line.

'Thank you, Joey,' Sophie said. 'I'm glad you enjoyed it.'

'I knew you were perfect for that part. This is your big break, Sophie. From now on, things are going to change for you, believe me! Listen, I think we can forget both John Payne and Franco Luciani.'

'You do?'

'Why should you work for peanuts? If you don't get a really outstanding offer in the next couple of weeks, then I've learned nothing in twenty years in this business!'

It was two hours before the phone calls slowed down, by which time she and Jenny were slightly tipsy, and feeling rather emotionally drained. The last call came at eleven, and was from Hélène le Bon, whom she hadn't seen for some months.

'Hélène!' Sophie exclaimed. 'It's lovely to hear from you! Are you still in Scotland?'

'No, I got back two days ago. I thought I'd wait until the rush was over before ringing you with my congratulations, darling. I presume the phone hasn't stopped ringing all evening?'

'Everyone's been so kind.' Sophie, who was herself starting to feel rather weepy by now, had to clear her throat. 'Anyway, as for congratulations, you're the one who deserves them most. You were brilliant.'

'I've been in this game a long time. For such a young actress, you achieved something remarkable in that film, Sophie. I hear on the grapevine that the job offers are flooding in.'

'Well, not exactly flooding,' Sophie smiled. 'I've had two offers to make films from directors I've never heard of.'

'Oh, I've heard of them both. In fact, I'm a great admirer of Franco Luciani. He's a very gifted young man, you know.'

'Is he?'

'You probably haven't seen *Roman Affair*, his last film? It wasn't exactly a box-office smash, but it was a very beautiful film. I was speaking to him only last week. He saw you in some of the unedited rushes, after Brighton—he has contacts in the drama studios.'

'I was wondering how he'd heard of me.'

'Well, he was very struck by the *Elmtree Road* footage. He seemed to think you had exactly the quality he was looking for in his next picture. He'll be even more struck now and, frankly, I couldn't think of two people who would go better together. Have you read his script?'

'Yes, I have.'

'What's it like?'

'It's very good. I didn't think it would suit me, but, having read it, I was seriously considering doing it.'

'In my humble opinion, darling, he's just the right man for you. I expect he isn't offering very much?'

'My agent thinks I can get more.'

'Darling, of course you could. But money isn't everything—certainly not in this game. Now, listen. We're having a little party tomorrow night. A lot of the cast from *The Elmtree Road Murders* will be there, and so will Franco Luciani. He's very keen to talk to you. Will you come and meet him?'

'I'd love to come!'

'Good. I'm so looking forward to talking to you. I think Franco Luciani is in for rather a surprise when he meets Maisie in the flesh!' Hélène laughed mischievously. 'He doesn't know that you don't look like Maisie any more.'

'I hope he doesn't want me to go through all that again,' Sophie groaned. 'I don't think I could!'

'He'll be quite happy with you as you are,' Hélène promised. 'The address is seventeen, Cadogan Gardens. Come around eight, and wear something shimmery. I'm dying to see you again. I've missed you.'

'I've missed you, too, Hélène. Oh, by the way—my cousin is staying with me at the moment——'

'Bring her with you, darling, of course. I'd love to meet her. What's her name?'

'Jenny.'

'Tell her I'm looking forward to talking to her. See you both tomorrow?'

Sophie rang off after a few words of goodbye, and told Jenny about the invitation.

'Oh, I'd *love* to meet Hélène le Bon in person! Will there be lots of gorgeous males?'

'I expect so,' Sophie nodded. 'Hélène knows everyone in the profession.'

She was definitely intrigued at the prospect of meeting Franco Luciani, the young Italian director who had taken such a fancy to her.

In the midst of her excitement, it suddenly occurred to her that there was someone else that she and Hélène had in common. Kyle.

Hélène would probably know where Kyle was, and what he was doing. She would be able to ask her tomorrow. If she dared.

If she dared? With a pang of grief, she realised that she couldn't go on like this, not any longer. She thought of nothing except Kyle, day and night, and if he didn't get in touch with her, she must get in touch with him.

She couldn't live in limbo. She had to know how he felt about her, whether he'd been serious in Jamaica, whether there was any chance of their getting together again.

If there wasn't—well, she would somehow have to come to terms with that. But she must know, one way or the other.

Her mind was made up. She would find out where Kyle was from Hélène tomorrow night, and then she would go and see him.

Cadogan Gardens, Sophie reflected the next evening, was exactly the right sort of address for someone like Hélène. Glitzy, expensive, central, it was just a stone's throw away from Sloane Square, located between some of the smartest schools in London and a set of Third World embassies.

Number seventeen had a beautiful neo-classical façade, and the pavement outside it was crowded with Rolls-Royces and Jaguars. All its windows were blazing, and the sound of music drifted through the summer evening. Hélène's 'little party' was obviously going to be a lavish affair.

Sophie paid the cab-driver, and they walked up the stairs together. Jenny was in one of Sophie's dark evening dresses, and looked, Sophie thought, ravishingly pretty in it, while Sophie herself had obeyed Hélène's order to wear 'something shimmery'. The silk blouse and metallic-print red skirt showed off her tan to perfection, and, though she was wearing the minimum of face-paint, as she had on that last night in Jamaica, she felt she looked as glamorous as she ever would.

They were met in the hall by Hélène herself, looking radiant, and obviously delighted to see them.

'Sophie, you look utterly delicious, darling! So brown and slim and lovely! Wait till the rest of them see you. And you never told me you had such a pretty cousin. So pleased to meet you, Jenny. Now come up, and have some champagne...'

The big drawing-room was crowded with people, talking and laughing, and Sophie's entrance caused a sudden uproar among the babble. For a breathless quarter of an hour she was enveloped by friends from the *Elmtree Road* set, congratulating her on her performance, and wide-eyed at the transformation she'd been through.

'I don't believe it,' Lionel Jakobson gasped. He had played one of Hélène's three husbands, and Sophie had got on well with him. His eyes, already rather bulging, were popping out of his florid face. 'We had no idea you looked like that under Maisie!'

'This is the Ugly Duckling turning into a swan, with a vengeance!' One of the other male leads, Julian Pike-Ashmore, made Sophie a mock obeisance. ' "You walk in beauty," my dear, "like the night Of cloudless climes and starry skies." May I beg a kiss?'

'Have you seen this?' one of the women asked, holding out a copy of *The Times*, folded open at the television page. The article about *The Elmtree Road Murders* was short, but enthusiastic. After praising the script and the director, Percy Schumaker, it went on to single out some of the performances, starting with Hélène's.

About Sophie, the writer said, 'The performance of newcomer Sophie Aspen, playing the difficult role of Maisie Wilkin, was one of the highlights of the film. She managed to combine the roles of victim and victimiser very convincingly. This young actress has a bright career ahead of her.'

Percy Schumaker himself was present, too, and came over to greet Sophie. He was very flattering about Sophie's contribution to the film's success, and dropped various hints about possible further opportunities to work with him in the coming year.

It was an exhilarating occasion, and Sophie had to leave her cousin to manage as best she could for a while— rather a new experience for Jenny, who was used to being the centre of attention.

After fifteen minutes Hélène approached, with a tall, olive-skinned man in tow. He was very handsome in a refined, rather sensitive way, and had intense, bright brown eyes. He smiled warmly as Hélène introduced him.

'Sophie, I want you to meet Franco Luciani. He wouldn't believe that you were really Sophie Aspen when he first saw you. Franco, you're face to face at last with Maisie Wilkin.'

'No. This is not Maisie Wilkin.' He had a charming accent, but spoke fluent English. 'This is somebody very different from Maisie Wilkin.' He kissed Sophie's hand, and held on to it in both of his as he straightened. 'I do not know which to compliment you on first, Sophie: your performance in *The Elmtree Road Murders*, or your appearance tonight.' His brown eyes gleamed appreciatively as he looked her up and down. 'May I say that both, in their way, are quite unique!'

'You're very kind,' Sophie laughed, colouring.

'I'll leave you to it,' Hélène said, melting away.

Sophie looked up shyly at the good-looking Italian. 'But you didn't think I really looked like Maisie, did you?' she asked.

'Well...' His full mouth curved into a smile. 'I knew you were heavily made-up. But I have to confess I didn't think you were so very beautiful, which I now see you are, or so charming, which I now also perceive.' He released her hand at last. 'When I saw the raw tapes of you playing Maisie Wilkin, I felt at once that you were the right actress to play Marjorie in *The First Day of Autumn*. My reaction to seeing those tapes was that an actress of your age who could play so difficult a role as Maisie could do anything. I was looking for someone young, and at the moment there is rather a shortage of gifted young actresses. You had the vulnerability, and yet the strength, that I wanted. But when I saw the full performance last night——' he shook his head '—it was breathtaking. During those final scenes, in the courtroom, I was holding on to my seat. One might almost have thought that you weren't an actress at all, but someone expressing a real hurt, a real anger.'

'Well,' Sophie said, thinking wryly of what had happened to bring out that performance, 'I'm glad I was convincing.'

'The only factor that bothered me was the Marjorie is meant to be very beautiful, while Maisie was...'

'Not very beautiful,' Sophie supplied, as he hesitated diplomatically.

Franco Luciani laughed quietly, showing even white teeth. 'Shall we say that Sophie Aspen is closer to my idea of Marjorie than Maisie was. With both talent and beauty on your side, I am more determined than ever that you must play Marjorie.'

'I'm very flattered,' Sophie murmured.

'Do you like the script?'

'Very much indeed,' she nodded. 'It's beautifully written, and I'm thinking about it very hard.'

'But even after three weeks of hard thinking, you are not willing to commit yourself just yet?'

She was rather taken aback by the full-frontal approach. 'Well, I'm still discussing it with my agent, and——'

'And he has advised you to wait and see whether you get a better offer?' He smiled with disarming frankness. 'And you are not sure about committing yourself to this almost-unknown Italian, whose films make no money, and who pays such low fees?'

'I can assure you that I'm not accustomed to high fees,' Sophie smiled. She was taking an instinctive liking to this man, 'And I am very flattered by your interest in me.'

'Have you other offers to consider?'

'Well—yes, I have.'

'Please, listen to me.' He took her hand in warm fingers, and looked intently into her face. 'On the strength of last night's showing, you could command much more money than I am offering. But I cannot raise my fee, much as I would like to. My finances are, as you no doubt know, very limited, and I am having to pay a great deal of money to get Luigi Canotta, the male lead. What I can do, however, is offer you a percentage of my share in the eventual box-office profits of *The First Day of Autumn*.'

'Mr Luciani——'

'That is something I have not offered Canotta. Sophie, I am convinced that this film will make money. It's different from *Roman Affair*, my last film. It's much more commercial, and much more contemporary. Your one or two per cent, whatever we decide on, could be worth a great deal more than the fee I'm offering. It could make money for you for years to come.'

'That's an extraordinarily generous offer, Mr Luciani, and I feel that . . .'

The words dried in Sophie's throat as her eyes fixed on someone over Franco's shoulder.

It was Kyle.

And Hélène le Bon, talking animatedly, was introducing him to Jenny.

Sophie felt that giant fist squeeze her heart tight as recognition slammed home. Her first thought was, He's been here, in London, and he hasn't contacted me!

Her second was to confirm her gut feeling, as though it needed confirming, that he was the most magnificent man she would ever see.

If anything even more tanned than she remembered from Jamaica, he was smiling lazily down at Jenny's coquettish, pretty face. His eyes were emerald slits between the smoky black lashes. The lithe, muscular body she remembered so well was sheathed in a dark silk suit tonight, the fine material doing no more than hint at the powerful shoulders and taut waist that had once lain naked against her own skin.

She laid her hand against her pounding heart, trying to catch the breath that seemed to have been seared from her lungs all of a sudden. Dimly, as if from far away, she was aware of Franco Luciani asking her something.

'I—I'm sorry.' She tore her hypnotised gaze away from Kyle and Jenny, and looked blindly at the director. 'What did you ask?'

He was frowning slightly. 'I asked whether you found that offer appealing. It's not uncommon these days, and many actors have found it a very profitable arrangement. Of course it's a gamble, but this is a gamble where you cannot actually lose money.'

'No, no, I find it a very interesting proposition,' she stammered, completely off balance. Suddenly, all she wanted to do was get away from Franco and speak to Kyle.

God, why did things work out like this? Just when she needed her concentration most——

'I will be working with a very small film unit,' Franco said. 'Almost impromptu. Costs will be very low. If you agreed to play Marjorie for me, we could bring the first day of shooting forward by two months. Canotta is free at this moment. We could be filming on location in Pisa by mid-September.'

'Mid-September? Next month?'

'Yes. Would that suit you?'

'It's a little short notice...but there's no reason why not.'

'Good,' Franco said, his expression easing. 'This is a film which will be made quickly and cleanly, without too much introspection. You understand me? Your part of it could be finished in less than eight weeks. At the most, ten weeks. The scenes between the hero and his family will be shot in the studios at Cinecittá, in Rome, later in the year. Once you'd finished in Pisa, you would be free to come back to London. Maybe we could even get the Pisa section shot in as little as six weeks. Why not? We have no special effects to contend with, a very small cast, and a relatively simple script. I have deliberately chosen to do it this way, to keep the expenses down. The problem with financing any kind of film in the present economic climate is that...'

Sophie wasn't listening any more. Her eyes had swung back to Kyle, now lifting his head to drain his champagne glass. Why didn't he look at her? He must know she was here! Was he deliberately ignoring her? Oh, look at me, she begged him silently, *please*...

Hélène had moved on to another group, leaving Kyle and Jenny talking. The silvery streaks at Kyle's tanned temples glinted as he turned to get Jenny another glass of champagne from a passing waiter. He smiled at her as he put it into her fingers, that formidably male face wearing its most deliberately charming mask.

And Jenny was moving into top gear, reacting to Kyle like a rose starting to bloom in the summer sunshine. A Venus's fly-trap, more likely, Sophie thought bitterly, catching Jenny's silvery laughter as Kyle murmured something amusing close to her ear.

She felt sick. Faced with Jenny's beauty, Kyle Hart's poised male experience was all too obvious; a slow smile was lurking on his lips, lips that she'd once imagined kissing so many women, leaving them all crying for more.

Something of Franco Luciani's passionate sincerity was making its way through her numbed thoughts. For God's sake, she cursed herself, one thing at a time. This man is making you a marvellous offer!

Once again, she dragged her eyes away from Kyle and tried to fix her mind on what the director was saying to her. 'Artistically, you find no obstacles about playing the part of Marjorie?'

'No, on the contrary, I think she's a wonderful character—— '

'And you are not, how do you say, put off by the difficulties of playing against an Italian lead? You don't speak any Italian, do you?'

'A—a little. I once did a course...'

'But that's wonderful,' Franco said, his eyes lighting up. He moved slightly, obscuring Kyle and hemming Sophie into a corner. 'When we start filming in Pisa...'

She tried to look interested in what Franco Luciani was saying, but the hollow, dizzy feeling inside wouldn't leave her alone. She tried to see round him, but he had stationed himself so as to monopolise her attention. Like other directors she had known, he was almost obsessive about his work, the project on hand dominating his thoughts to the exclusion of all others.

It washed over her like rain, and it was twenty agonising minutes before the director interrupted his own monologue. 'But this is not the time or place to talk business,' he said. 'I simply wanted to give you some time to think about the idea.'

'Your offer is extremely generous,' she said, trying to smile. 'I'd very much like to discuss it with Joey Gilmour, my agent. I'm no good at business, I'm afraid—he deals with all that side of it for me—— '

'Of course. We will arrange a more formal meeting to discuss the details.' He leaned close to her. 'And do not forget, what could be worth even more than that is the chance to star in a film that attracts attention. Believe me, Sophie Aspen, *The First Day of Autumn* will attract a great deal of attention.' He straightened his back proudly. 'I have made commercially unsuccessful films, but I have never made a bad film.'

'I'm ashamed to say I haven't seen *Roman Affair*,' Sophie said, 'but everyone speaks very highly of your work.' She touched his arm. 'I'm terribly sorry,' she said awkwardly, 'this is absolutely fascinating, but I've just remembered something important I must say to my cousin. Could you excuse me for ten minutes?'

'Of course,' he beamed, evidently delighted at finding Sophie in such a receptive mood. He helped himself to a glass of champagne as Sophie started across the room to where Kyle and Jenny were standing.

CHAPTER SIX

KYLE was a head taller than most of the men in the room, his dark presence seeming, in Sophie's eyes at least, to dominate everyone else. Her heart was in her mouth, her palms clammy with perspiration, as she approached through the crowd. How was he going to treat her?

'Hello, Kyle,' Sophie said softly. As on a previous meeting, her throat was constricted. She found speech with an effort. 'How are you?'

Kyle's gaze swung her way, but there wasn't a flicker of emotion on his face as their eyes met. 'Fine,' he said with cool politeness. 'And you?'

Sophie felt as though someone had just dashed a bucket of iced water in her face.

'Fine.'

'Do you two know each other?' Jenny said, looking slightly put out.

'We've met,' Kyle said huskily.

'Don't tell me you're another member of the Sophie Aspen fan club,' Jenny groaned. 'All I've heard tonight is how wonderful my theatrical cousin is. Did you watch *The Elmtree Road Murders* last night?'

He shook his head, and Jenny brightened. 'I was tied up with a friend.' He put just enough emphasis on 'friend' to leave no doubt that he meant a lady friend. 'But I understand that Sophie's performance was something special.'

'I've never seen anything like it,' Jenny snickered. 'You really missed something, Kyle.'

'The story of my life,' he said, with a cold smile. 'What was so special about it?'

123

'Oh, Sophie's make-up was just amazing.' Jenny's eyes were bright with malicious laughter. 'I couldn't stop laughing. She looked like . . . well, like nothing on earth.'

'Really?' Kyle drawled. 'How bizarre.'

'*Grotesque* would be a better word. I couldn't believe it when I saw her,' Jenny gushed. 'I said I wouldn't have let anyone make me look as awful as that for a thousand pounds! You couldn't imagine it, Kyle.'

'Perhaps I could.' Ice-green eyes were holding Sophie's. 'As a matter of fact, I last met your cousin in Brighton, during the filming of *The Elmtree Road Murders*, and she presented a very different picture then.'

'Then you haven't seen Sophie since she was playing Maisie?' Jenny asked, wide-eyed. 'Gosh, you must hardly recognise her.'

'I see her with new eyes,' Kyle agreed, but only Sophie caught the razor's edge that lay beneath the bland words.

'Doesn't it surprise you to find how *beautiful* Sophie really is?' Jenny said, with just enough of a droop of her eyelashes to utterly devalue the statement.

Sophie knew this routine of Jenny's so well, and yet it never ceased to make her wilt. Jenny was an expert at putting her down in the presence of any remotely attractive male. No matter how close they were, as relations and as friends, when a desirable man was involved Jenny suddenly turned into an utterly ruthless bitch, for whom no hold was barred.

Kyle's gaze left Sophie's face at last, and moved down the length of her body with cool assessment. 'You've changed since then,' he said drily. 'I might not have recognised you, Sophie.'

'Yes,' she said numbly, 'I've changed since Brighton——'

'You're another woman,' he said flatly.

By now she knew, with no shadow of a doubt, that Kyle hadn't forgiven her, wasn't going to forgive her. Yet she could not resist probing further, as though there might still be a chance . . .

She found the words with an effort. 'But we've met since Brighton, Kyle.'

'Have we?' he raised a negligent eyebrow. 'I'm afraid I must have forgotten.'

She shook her head at him slightly, fighting down the pain. 'I remember it well.'

'How odd!' Jenny, picking up the tension, had scented something juicy. 'Where was that, Sophie?'

'We bumped into each other once or twice,' Sophie said dully, feeling despair unfold leaden wings inside her.

'Yes,' Jenny persisted, 'but how come Kyle didn't know who you were?'

'Your cousin is such a very talented young actress,' Kyle said ironically, watching Sophie with ice-green eyes. 'Who knows, perhaps I didn't recognise her. Where did we "bump into each other", Sophie?'

'If you don't remember,' Sophie said distantly, 'then it hardly matters.'

'But I'm curious,' Kyle said with a cold smile. 'And you've got your cousin intrigued. Do remind me of the occasion.'

Colour was starting to rise hotly into Sophie's face. 'We met in Jamaica,' she forced herself to say.

'In Jamaica?' Kyle was wearing an expression of cool surprise. 'But, my dear Sophie, I remember nothing about this meeting. I spent quite some time there, and I certainly don't recall meeting any Sophie Aspen.'

Jenny had been following this exchange with bright, inquisitive eyes. Kyle now turned the full force of his smile on her. 'How delicious to see two such beautiful women together,' he drawled. 'You might almost be sisters. Sophie told me about you.'

'Did she?' Jenny preened.

'She told me you had beauty as well as brains, and I now see that she was understating the case.' He gave Jenny a slow, appreciative once-over. 'Yet your cousin gets all the attention.'

'Oh, we have different talents,' Jenny answered with a bright laugh. 'We've never competed.'

'Except for men?' Kyle suggested gently.

'Oh, Kyle,' Jenny said breathily, 'I've *never* had to compete with my cousin for men.'

'I can see why not,' Kyle said meaningfully. 'What a waste for someone as radiant as you to be closeted in the dusty realms of mathematics.'

This was music to Jenny's ears. She glanced triumphantly at a silent Sophie. 'Oh, maths isn't all that dusty. As if happens, I spend most of my time working with a giant computer which positively gleams with cleanliness.'

'In a laboratory where no one sees your beauty. I wonder whether your professors appreciate the loveliness that is under their noses?' His voice was tantamount to a caress, and Sophie watched the coquettish droop of her cousin's eyelashes.

'As it happens,' Jenny said mischievously, 'some are more appreciative than others.'

Kyle arched one eyebrow. 'I thought that sort of thing didn't go on.'

'It goes on,' Jenny said with heavy innuendo, 'believe me.'

'Ah,' Kyle said softly. 'Well, that doesn't surprise me. You must be a devastating temptation.'

They were ignoring Sophie completely. She was standing like a fool, transfixed with the sick hollowness inside. Jenny's eyes were glowing as she basked in Kyle's attention. 'Anyway,' she said, 'as a banker, you must be something of a mathematician yourself, Kyle?'

'Oh, yes. The purity of applied maths has always interested me. Numbers cannot lie. They can't deceive or cheat, or pretend to be something they're not.'

'But that's exactly what I love about mathematics!' Jenny exclaimed. 'I love the way it's all so unambiguous. There's always an answer, or almost always. Life isn't like that.'

'No,' Kyle said. His eyes glittered at Sophie. 'Life isn't like that, and people aren't like that. I detest dishonesty, above all else. It sickens me.'

Sophie's heart was pounding painfully against her breast-bone. It was far worse than she'd dreamed. He wasn't just indifferent to her. She knew Kyle well enough to sense the radiating anger that blazed beneath his impeccable façade. There was no question of his forgiving her for what she'd done in Jamaica. He was, she knew with sudden certainty, intent on making her pay.

'Don't you agree, Sophie?' he challenged meaningfully.

'Perhaps,' she said in a low voice. 'But numbers don't have hearts. A thing without a heart can never lie. On the other hand, it can't love, either, or be loved in return.'

Kyle took Jenny's arm casually. 'Do you agree with that?' he asked.

'Well,' Jenny said, almost purring at the contact, 'I'm no expert on true love. Personally, I reckon it's a lot of irrelevant sentimental idiocy. I prefer straightforward relationships...' she looked at Kyle from under thick lashes '... without emotional strings.'

'My opinions exactly,' Kyle said, looking into Jenny's eyes with a dark smile. 'You and I have much in common, Jenny.'

Sophie couldn't stand it any longer. She turned to Jenny pleadingly. 'Jenny,' she said in a quiet voice, 'would you give me a moment alone with Kyle?'

Jenny looked angrily back at Sophie. 'What?'

'I want a private word with Kyle. Just a few minutes.'

'Well, I really think——'

'Please.'

'But don't go far,' Kyle said, giving Jenny another smoky smile. 'I'm sure your cousin won't detain me for long.'

Jenny flounced off indignantly, and stood sulking by the drinks trolley. Sophie looked up into the tanned, rugged face that had haunted her dreams. 'I tried to ring you, the day I got back to England, but you'd already checked out. Why didn't you get in touch with me?' she asked in a low voice.

'Did you really expect me to?' Kyle asked contemptuously, not bothering to keep up the urbane manner now that Jenny was no longer present.

'I thought that after what happened between us in Jamaica...'

'What happened between us?' He spoke with such concentrated venom that Sophie dropped her gaze. 'You astonish me, Sophie,' he rasped. 'After that despicable little charade in Jamaica, I find it incredible that you have the face to even approach me.'

She gasped slightly at the force of his anger. 'Kyle, please listen to me,' she begged. 'I didn't want it to be a charade. But I found myself in a corner. I didn't know how to get out of it——'

'You two-faced little fake,' he cut through harshly. 'You're the cheapest swindler I've met in a lifetime of dealing with cheap swindlers.'

The colour was draining from Sophie's face. 'That's cruel and unfair——'

'Wasn't what you did to me cruel and unfair?' The skin around his eyes was tight with anger. 'I wonder how all your admiring friends would feel about you if I made a speech about your gifts, right now? Would they still respect you once they knew about the fine performance you gave in Jamaica, for the benefit of your captive audience?'

'It started out as a performance,' Sophie said, struggling to keep her composure. 'But it didn't end up that way.'

He laughed shortly. 'You've had your little game with me,' he said. 'But the game is now over. Don't drag it out any further.'

She was white. 'It isn't a game, not to me!'

'But it's a game to me.' His smile was arctic. 'It's *my* game now.'

'What do you mean?'

'I mean that, as you hurt me, I intend to hurt you.'

'Oh, Kyle,' she said quietly. 'I told you you were a typical Scorpio, didn't I?'

'So you did,' he said silkily. 'Did you think you could just walk all over my pride, and get away with it?'

'You once walked all over my pride,' she shot back. 'If you had any idea how you hurt me in Brighton——'

'You eavesdropped on a conversation you half understood in Brighton.' His passionate mouth curled. 'I don't know what you heard that afternoon, but I would never have said anything unkind about you to your face. I never set out to hurt you. But you set out to hurt *me*. Your vanity was piqued, so you thought you would get your own back. You decided to make a fool of me, the most complete fool you could manage.'

'That's a distortion of the truth!' Her grey eyes were misty with pain. 'You didn't recognise me when we met that day on the beach. I waited to see whether you would remember who I was, but you didn't——'

'And you helped jog my memory, of course, by giving yourself a false name and lying to me about your job.'

'I just wanted to tease you. I never planned it to go so far!' She was begging him to believe what she was saying. 'I had no idea we would get so close——'

'Or that we would wind up in bed?' he finished for her. 'God, I was a fool. A blind fool. There was something about you that haunted me, from the moment we met—but I never suspected the truth.' His eyes burned into hers. 'Three weeks. You had me going for three damned weeks! You must have found it so entertaining, watching me falling for you, watching me get caught in your web!'

'It wasn't like that,' she answered shakily. 'But if it comes to that, didn't *you* once find it amusing that I had fallen for *you*?'

His fingers clamped painfully around Sophie's bare arm, making her gasp with shock. 'I never did what you did,' he grated. 'You let me take you to bed, let me make love to you, let me tell you how wonderful you were, how much I cared about you—and all the time you were laughing yourself sick behind your hand!'

'No! It wasn't like that! If you only knew how much I've regretted the way it all ended. But I didn't know what else to do!'

'The only thing you've regretted is that you weren't there to watch my face as I read your clever little letter,' he retorted. His anger was turning back into cold dislike again. He released her arm at last, and if her skin hadn't been so tanned his fingers would have left livid marks on her flesh. 'You would have had a most amusing spectacle,' he said, with a cold smile. 'I felt as though the earth had caved in under my feet. That's what you wanted, wasn't it?'

She wiped her tear-soaked lashes tremblingly. 'Oh, no, Kyle——'

'You play very dirty, Sophie,' he said bitterly. 'But you'll find I can play dirty, too.'

'Is that why you came here tonight?' she asked unsteadily. 'To tell me all this?'

'I didn't come to see you at all,' he retorted with a tiger's smile. 'I came to see someone else.'

'What do you mean?' she followed his eyes, and found herself staring at Jenny, who was now talking to another man. An icy chill flooded her veins as she looked back into Kyle's hard, unforgiving eyes. 'Jenny? You came to see Jenny?'

'Why not? Your sweet little cousin and I have a lot in common, hadn't you gathered that? We both prefer uncomplicated relationships without falsehood or irrelevant emotions.'

'You don't even know her!'

'That can be rectified,' he said lazily. 'She tells me she's in London for the next three weeks. That is exactly the right period for my purposes. I intend to get to know your cousin very well indeed during the coming three weeks.' His eyes travelled appreciatively down Jenny's slender figure. 'She even looks like you. You were right, of course, she's far prettier than you'll ever be. But the resemblance is there, and that will give me added pleasure.'

'What do you mean, added pleasure?'

'When I taste what was denied me in Jamaica.'

Shock made Sophie numb for a moment as his meaning dawned on her. 'I don't believe you,' she whispered. 'You wouldn't do that!'

'Why wouldn't I?'

'Kyle, no! Having an affair with Jenny isn't a fit pastime for a man like you!'

'You are a very poor judge of what is fit, and what isn't,' he retorted mockingly. 'Since you obviously have no honour or pride to hurt, Sophie, I must hurt you through whatever means I can find.' He tilted his head to look down at her dispassionately. 'When Hélène told me your cousin was staying with you, I remembered what you once told me. About your jealousy and resentment of Jenny. You weren't lying to me about that, were you? After all, Jenny is so much prettier than you. So much sexier, too.'

'Kyle,' she said in horror, 'for God's sake!'

'Yes,' he smiled drily. 'I see I was right. Jealousy is one of the few emotions you're vulnerable to. Like most actresses, your pride is your Achilles' heel.'

Unbearable hurt made her feel physically sick. 'How could you think of something as sadistic as that?' she whispered.

'I call it justice,' he replied softly.

'I'll stop you. I'll tell Jenny. I'll—I'll tell her what happened in Jamaica!'

'Do. Tell her just what a bitch you've been. I'm sure she'll be most edified to hear all about it.'

'Jenny would never do anything to hurt me!'

'Wouldn't she?' His expression was amused. 'I think she would. I think Jenny takes a particular pleasure in stealing men from you. She does steal all your favourite men, doesn't she?'

'God,' she whispered, 'why did I ever tell you that?'

'One look into your cousin's eyes tells me just how different she is from you. That, unlike you, she has the ability to please a man, and be pleased in return.' Sophie stared up into the magnificent, cold face, her blood like ice. 'Tell Jenny all about it,' he invited smoothly. 'Tell her what you did to me in Jamaica, then tell her that I'm going to have an affair with her. See if that puts her off. She'll enjoy it as much as I will. And I'll enjoy it very much.' He reached out tauntingly, and caressed her half-open, velvety mouth. 'Your pride is going to take rather a pounding, my dear Sophie. How will it feel to watch your younger, prettier, sexier cousin get the man you betrayed? Perhaps, when you think of Jenny in my arms, you might regret that little trick you played on me in Ocho Rios!'

'Please,' she whispered, her eyes blurring. 'Please don't do this.'

'It's easy to see why she stole your men. The two of you are like gold and lead. She is the gold, but you, Sophie, are lead. Cold, grey, uninteresting. She's not just more attractive. She's sexually receptive. You are not.' He said it with biting disdain. 'You're clearly incapable of a normal relationship with any man. That's really why you had to go through that incredibly elaborate sham in Jamaica, isn't it? You prefer fiction to reality. What are you so afraid of? That one day a man will find out just how colourless and frigid you really are?'

Sophie was staring at him in horror, silenced. With a last cruel smile into Sophie's eyes, Kyle turned and walked over to Jenny, taking her arm and murmuring something into her ear.

And Franco Luciani, spotting that Sophie was alone, chose that moment to come back over to her. His big, intense eyes searched her face.

'Are you all right, Sophie?' he demanded, looking at her curiously. 'You've gone very pale.'

'I'm fine,' she nodded dizzily, and took an unsteady breath. 'Perhaps the—the champagne went to my head—a little.'

Franco nodded. 'Can we get back to what we were talking about a few minutes ago? I'd be extremely interested to hear your views on the character of Marjorie. How did you read the part?'

Sophie tried to stir her bruised mind into some kind of reply. Dissociated from the empty words that came from her mouth, her thoughts were fraught with pain. *What could she do?*

The answer was nothing. Just brace herself for the crushing blow of seeing the man she loved walk into a shallow, deliberate affair with her cousin.

And Kyle was right. The idea of her, a virgin, being any sort of competition for Jenny was absurd. Despite the two-year age-gap between them, Jenny was infinitely more experienced with men than she would ever be. Infinitely more experienced, and infinitely more attractive.

She felt a wave of acute sickness, as though she'd just been struck in the solar plexus.

Some part of her mind must have been functioning independently of her inner thoughts, because although she had not the faintest idea of what she'd been saying to Franco Luciani, he nodded eagerly.

'That is very profound. You have hit on the essential element in the character of Marjorie. She is a woman in the grip of an addiction stronger than she knows how to deal with. She finds love, but that cannot save her. She embraces the flames that devour her——'

'Sorry to interrupt.' It was Jenny, her blue eyes sapphire-bright as she came over to talk to Sophie. She gave

Franco a pretty smile, and drew her cousin aside. 'Kyle wants me to go to a nightclub with him.'

'Now?' Sophie asked in pain.

'This is your party,' Jenny sneered. 'I don't know a soul here. And Kyle's as bored as I am. Frankly, I'd far rather be dancing with him. Do you mind?'

Sophie fought for control. 'No,' she said, almost inaudibly, 'of course I don't mind.'

Jenny leaned forward, 'God, isn't he fantastic?' she giggled under her breath. 'He's the best-looking man I've ever seen in my *life*, and he's obviously on the loose. I can't believe my luck! Why haven't you told me about him?'

'I—I don't know.'

'What's between you?' Jenny's blue eyes were eager, greedy. 'Have you had an affair with him? I mean, I'm not poaching, am I? I'd hate to be taking yet *another* man from you.'

'There's nothing between us,' Sophie said, feeling as though she were in the grip of some icy paralysis.

'Good,' Jenny sparkled wickedly. 'Because I have very good feelings about tonight. He's got that certain look in his eyes. So don't wait up for me!'

'Jenny,' Sophie pleaded, her eyes as dark as her cousin's were brilliant, 'don't...'

'Don't what?' Her cousin's smile was unmistakably taunting.

'Just—just be careful.'

'Not a chance,' Jenny grinned. 'Kyle Hart isn't the kind of man a woman should be careful with. That was always your trouble, darling. Not knowing when to go for it. Well, good luck with your Italian; he's pretty yummy, too. Bye!'

'What a pretty girl,' Franco said appreciatively, as Jenny hurried off. 'She's younger than you, isn't she?'

'Yes,' Sophie said. The room was blurring around her, only isolated details coming through the haze. Kyle's eyes, meeting hers in cold triumph. His arm sliding round

Jenny's waist as they headed discreetly for the door. The
distant laughter of Hélène le Bon. The sound of pulsing
music—or was it her own blood, pounding in her ears?

'Sophie, you look ill,' Franco said, peering at her.
'Sophie?'

'I'm sorry,' she tried to say, 'I'd better sit down...'

Franco was just in time to take her in his arms as she
sagged against him, darkness flooding her mind.

She awoke late the next morning, feeling panicky and
depressed.

Memories of last night flooded in. Where was Jenny?
She got up quickly, and pulled on her dressing-gown,
then padded out into the corridor in her bare feet.

She pushed the door of her tiny guest bedroom quietly
open, and peeped in.

The immaculate bed hadn't been slept in. Sophie
fought down the tears as she sagged against the doorway.
Jenny had not come home last night. Where she was
now was anybody's guess. Especially Kyle's.

Gathering her strength, she went into the bathroom
and showered. Last night drifted through her thoughts
as she stood under the spray. What a débâcle. Coming
out of her faint with a crowd of anxious faces round
her. Hélène's concerned eyes and kind words. People
blaming the heat, or the champagne, or the excitement.
People offering to take her home. Nobody understanding a thing...

Stupidly, she'd kept on announcing that she was fine,
and that she wanted to stay on, when all the time she'd
just wanted to run a hundred miles away, and bury her
pain and humiliation somewhere out of sight. The rest
of the evening had been stretched and hazy, like someone
on the rack, until Franco Luciani had eventually taken
pity on her glazed eyes and white face, and had insisted
on driving her home.

She'd never taken a sleeping-pill in her life, but last
night she'd wanted one badly.

Come to think of it, she could have crawled back into bed right now, and buried her head in misery...

She had to keep reminding herself that although Jenny was enjoying her latest triumph, she was completely innocent of Kyle's darker purpose, completely ignorant of the relationship Kyle had once had with her.

Jenny could cope with most situations. Sophie couldn't. Maybe Kyle had been right about her. Maybe she wasn't able to have a normal relationship with a man. Maybe that *was* why she'd invented that elaborate charade in Jamaica.

Whatever the truth of it, Kyle was going to make her pay, all right. He'd worked out a torment of hell for her.

How could a man who'd once felt so much for her now be so cruel and vindictive? She'd once thought him shallow. God! Could she ever have been more mistaken? She'd never guessed at the depth of his feelings, had never known a tenth of how deeply he'd really felt about her...

She was making a cup of coffee half an hour later when Hélène rang.

'How are you feeling? Any better?'

'Much better,' Sophie lied, trying to sound sincere. 'I slept like a log.'

'Did something upset you last night?'

'Oh, no.' She fell back on the well-worn excuse. 'It's just not a very good time of the month for me.'

'I see! Well, I'm glad that's what it was, darling. I was worried. I saw you talking to Kyle, and I wondered whether you might have been distressed by something he said or did. I couldn't help noticing...well, that he left the party early with your cousin, Jenny.'

'Yes,' Sophie said with an effort. 'They went to a nightclub together.'

'Did they have a good time?'

'Jenny didn't—didn't come home last night. She's not back yet.'

'I see,' Hélène said quietly. 'I think I can imagine how you feel.' Sophie was silent, and Hélène went on quickly, 'It seemed to me, last year in Brighton, that you grew rather fond of Kyle. I don't want to seem as though I'm prying, but you were obviously very taken with him. It's just that I didn't think your feelings would still be so strong, all this time later—otherwise I would never have asked him to the party. It must be nine months since you last met him.'

'No,' Sophie said wearily. 'We've met since then.'

'I didn't know that.'

'It was in Jamaica...' Sophie struggled to find words to describe what had happened between her and Kyle. But it now seemed so unreal, so impossible to explain.

'While you were on holiday?' Hélène prompted.

'Yes. Oh, Hélène, I've been such a fool. I did something so stupid to him, really hurt his pride, and now...now he hates me.'

'I don't believe that!' Hélène exclaimed. 'Kyle always had a very soft spot for you. And when I say that, I'm talking about a man who has very few soft spots—especially for women.'

'He found me ridiculous in Brighton. And I *was* ridiculous.' Her voice trembled slightly. 'And now that I'm presentable, I've gone and wrecked everything in another way.'

'Kyle didn't find you altogether ridiculous.' Hélène was silent for a moment. Then she asked quietly, 'You overheard us that day, on the beach, didn't you?'

'Yes,' Sophie said dully. 'I didn't mean to, but it just happened that way.'

'I thought you must have heard something. You were so cold to him over those last few days. You treated him as though he'd suddenly stopped existing. As a matter of interest, what *did* you hear?'

'I heard Kyle telling you how...how amusing he found it that I was so obviously infatuated with him. He said a lot of other things, about the way I looked and dressed.

About what a spectacle I was. He was asking you to speak to me about my appearance.'

'Oh, dear. Is that all you heard?'

'Well . . . I didn't stay very long.'

Hélène sighed. 'You didn't hear him say how charming he found you as a person? Or how he admired your acting ability? Or what good company you were?'

'He seemed to think the way I looked was more important.'

'Kyle knew very little about you, then. He didn't know that you had changed your appearance radically to play the part of Maisie. No one had told him that. The afternoon you overheard us, he was asking me about you, and I was explaining how Percy had insisted on the slatternly image for Maisie, and that it wasn't really you.'

'What did he say?'

Hélène laughed softly. 'He said that he couldn't wait to see you once you'd gone back to normal. How did he react when he met you in Jamaica?'

'He . . . he didn't recognise me.'

'I'm not surprised,' Hélène smiled.

'No, you don't understand,' Sophie said tautly. 'He *never* recognised me. You see, he wanted me. I thought he was just making a pass at first, and I thought I'd tease him a little. I lied to him about my name, and just let him go on thinking that he'd never met me before.'

'Oh, Sophie! But *why*?'

'I suppose I must have wanted to get back at him in some way. Prove a point, maybe. But . . . things changed so quickly. I think he was really serious at the end, and I just didn't know how to handle it any more. I behaved so badly. The day I left Jamaica, I wrote him a note explaining who I was. A really stupid, childish note. But by then I was so involved with him. I don't know what made me behave in that way, but I regret it so much now! That's why he's so disgusted with me, Hélène.'

'Oh, Sophie!' Hélène mourned. 'How could you have been so silly?'

'I've been sitting here for three weeks asking myself just that, and praying he would get back in touch with me. I didn't realise how angry he was. Last night he...he said such cutting things to me. And he only went out with Jenny to hit back at me. He seems determined to punish me for what I did.' Sophie's voice broke. 'What can I do?'

Hélène paused for a long while, as though thinking. 'I don't know what you can do,' she said slowly at last. 'But I want to tell you something about Kyle Hart. I've known him a long time, and I consider him a good friend. He's an achiever, Sophie. He was a little wild in his early twenties, but he settled down after a year or two in the Caribbean. Did he tell you about that?'

'A little bit,' Sophie nodded.

'Well, he's done absolutely brilliantly since then. He's made a fortune for his bank, and he's now one of the most powerful men, for his age, in the City. He's been responsible for countless projects, and he's very highly thought of. Kyle works incredibly hard at his job, and he plays hard, too. With women . . . well, I don't need to tell you that he just has to whistle. He's had a succession of the most stunning girlfriends, and none of them ever seem to have meant much to him. Do I sound as though I'm rubbing it in?'

'A little,' Sophie said wryly.

'Well, I'm trying to make a point. The point is that, for all his success with our sex, Kyle is very wary. Whether he's had some bad experiences, or whether it's just constitutional, I don't know. But he's erected some formidable defences, and he tends to be very distrustful of any woman who looks like breaching them. Any time one of his girlfriends seems to be getting close to him, the barrier suddenly comes down, and they're excluded. I've seen it happen half a dozen times. Sometimes they come to me in tears and ask me what they did wrong, and I have to say I simply don't know. I've always guessed that Kyle simply wants happy, mainly sexual relationships with his women, without involvement or commitment on either side. The unfortunate thing,' she added with a little sigh, 'is that he's the kind of man very few women can treat like that. They tend to fall in love with him. Hard.'

'It isn't difficult to do,' Sophie said drily.

'No, I suppose not. What I'm getting around to, darling, is that you seem to be the one exception that proves the rule. It sounds to me as though you actually did get through his defences. You've probably seen a side of Kyle that he's shown to very, very few women. As I said,' Hélène commented gently, 'he always did have a very soft spot for you. But as it's turned out ... well, you've probably hurt him far more deeply than you guessed at the time.'

'Oh, no,' Sophie said in dawning horror.

'He's also probably very angry. And when he's angry, he's capable of hitting out with a great deal of force. I can't tell you how to run your life, but I really don't think you have much to gain by trying to face up to him. You'll only collect a lot of unnecessary bruises. Do you want me to talk to him?'

'No, please don't. It wouldn't make things any better.'

'No, I don't think it would. I'll do what I can, without actually interfering. Sophie, I know this is going to hurt, but I've never known Kyle go back to anyone whom he's once cut out of his life. He's a very decisive man. If he's striking up a relationship with your cousin, then it's going to be murder for you to stand by and watch, but there really isn't anything you can do. Except try and get over it, and remember that Jenny is probably far less vulnerable to Kyle than you are.'

Hélène spoke a great deal more, but after that Sophie's mind was numb. How was she ever going to adjust to the truths she had learned this morning?

The things Kyle had said to her in Ocho Rios, things she'd thought he said to every woman he wanted ... he'd really meant them. He wasn't the kind of man to talk to a woman like that, not casually.

'You're a very special woman, my love. I just know we've met before. But if it wasn't in this lifetime, then it must have been in some other one, because I feel that I'm acquainted with you. The important thing is that we don't lose one another again.'

And she'd been so blasé, so cool with him.

'That kind of talk is for shallow people—not persons of deep feeling, like you and I.'

He'd felt something special for her, and she had thrown it back in his face. Had insanely thrown away the rarest gift that Kyle could give a woman—his trust. And she would never get it back again.

It was almost ten-thirty that morning by the time she heard Jenny's key in the door. And Kyle was with her.

They were both still in last night's evening clothes, and Kyle's arm was possessively round Jenny's waist as they came into the little flat, laughing. They brought with them a scent of perfume, whisky and cigars.

'God, we've had such a fabulous time,' Jenny said with a giggle, collapsing into an armchair beside Sophie and throwing her red-gold hair back. She looked like a cat who'd just had a bowl of double cream all to itself.

'Have you?' Sophie asked brightly, avoiding meeting Kyle's mocking green eyes. 'Where did you go?'

'Oh, I can hardly remember.' Jenny yawned lazily, showing a pink inner mouth. 'To a disco, first. What was that place called, darling?'

'La Valbonne,' Kyle said, leaning negligently against the mantelpiece. His presence seemed to overpower the tiny flat, making Sophie feel as though she were being crushed into a corner. 'Not exactly your scene, Sophie.'

'I'll say not,' Jenny agreed maliciously. 'Bit too wild for you. But it was *fabulous*,' she sighed. 'We even had a swim in the pool. Then we had dinner at the Café Royal. I've never seen so many celebrities! The place was wall-to-wall film stars and pop stars. Then we went

to La Capanina, and danced practically till dawn...
We've just had breakfast at the Dorchester!'

Sophie forced a smile. 'And where did you go between
dawn and the Dorchester?'

'You wouldn't believe us if we told you,' Jenny
gurgled, her blue eyes sparkling.

An agonising flash of memory seared Sophie's mind,
as she recalled what she herself had once got up to with
Kyle in the early hours of the morning. 'No,' she agreed
drily, hiding her pain under a composed face, 'I probably
wouldn't.' She grasped after normality with a supreme
effort. 'Would either of you like a cup of coffee?'

'Love one,' Jenny nodded. 'And you, darling?'

Kyle glanced at his watch, the black diver's watch she
remembered so well. 'Why not?' he agreed easily. 'I don't
have any appointments until noon.'

Jenny jumped to her feet. 'I'm going to have a
lightning shower while you put the percolator on,
Sophie.' She stroked Kyle's cheek. 'You don't mind,
darling?'

That made three darlings so far, Sophie noted sav-
agely. She walked stiffly to the kitchen, praying that Kyle
wouldn't end up making her hate her own cousin.

She started making coffee in a state of blind tension,
her fingers clumsy and disobedient. From the bathroom
came the sound of Jenny showering.

'So this is where you live.' She turned. Kyle was
watching her from the doorway, his dark face amused.
He glanced around without bothering to disguise his
disdain. 'Rather a poky little place.'

'It's all I can afford!' Sophie snapped, scattering coffee
as she filled the percolator. 'Unlike you, I don't own my
own bank.'

'How did you sleep last night?'

'Fine—*darling*.'

'Really?' he drawled. 'You seem kind of ragged this
morning.'

'I obviously don't have your stamina for night-life,' she replied bitterly.

'A little birdie tells me,' he said gently, 'that you threw a fainting fit at Hélène's last night. Right after I left the party with your cousin.'

'I was tired,' she said stiffly. 'I got a little giddy.'

'Nothing to do with me and Jenny?' Silent laughter sparkled in his eyes as he watched her. 'My, my. That really must have hit you hard. I hear that Luciani was most impressed.' He mimicked the Italian's accent with wicked accuracy. '"Thees ees exactly what I want for my wonderful new film."'

'Very amusing,' Sophie bit out.

'You're good at doing emotional scenes, aren't you?' he mocked. 'Everyone keeps telling me what a brilliant performance you put in at the end of *The Elmtree Road Murders*. They say the final scenes were quite stunning. I'm starting to be sorry I didn't catch it, but I was very much occupied that night. With a ladyfriend.'

That soft postscript hurt like a barb in her flesh. 'So you've already said. I'm sure you were much better occupied,' she said, pretending indifference. 'But if I did act competently, then part of the credit must go to you.'

He arched one dark eyebrow. 'Indeed?'

'If I hadn't been brought down to earth with a bump one afternoon, I might not have put in such a realistic performance,' she informed him lightly.

'Well, well.' He subjected her to a slow, deliberate scrutiny. 'What happened in Brighton really seems to bother you. You had quite a crush on me then, didn't you?'

The sudden, hectic flush on her cheeks emphasised her paleness. 'I really don't remember.'

'I do. It was painfully obvious.'

'Yes, I should have been much more discreet about my juvenile feelings, shouldn't I?' She gave him a tight smile. 'But unfortunately, I didn't know just how...absurd you found me.'

Kyle smiled drily. 'Want to hear something funny?'

'I could do with a laugh.'

'I liked you in Brighton, Sophie. I liked you a lot. You amused me, really you did. I had the idea that we might become good friends.'

She looked down. 'Is that ... all?'

'A good friend is a much rarer and more precious commodity than a good lover,' he assured her ironically. 'But it seemed it was not to be.'

'You said awful things about me,' she told him in a low voice. 'Things that hurt me for months afterwards.'

'You weren't meant to hear them,' he retorted. 'And not many people can afford to eavesdrop on what others say about them, and not be hurt. I didn't understand the role you were playing, until Hélène explained about it. I thought you were just being sloppy. I didn't know then how much you were throwing yourself into your part.' He paused. 'As I remember it, that afternoon I was being rather clever about your evident infatuation with me.'

'Yes,' she said dully.

'I never understood why you changed towards me so abruptly. I didn't guess what had happened. I just got the message that my company was suddenly not welcome any longer. But of course, you were already plotting your little revenge, weren't you?'

She lit the gas, and put the percolator on. In the silence, they heard the shower stop. Jenny was humming gaily as she dried herself.

'As a matter of interest,' Sophie asked, 'what *did* you do between dawn and breakfast?'

'I took your sweet little cousin to bed.'

The teaspoons clattered out of Sophie's paralysed fingers into the sink. The world swayed dizzily around her as her eyes flooded with tears.

'Oh, Kyle,' she whispered numbly, staring at his blurred figure. 'You didn't!'

He looked at her grief-stricken face for a moment, then laughed huskily. 'Oh, but I did—*darling*.' Sophie felt so sick that she thought she might throw up. Then Kyle went on, 'However, I didn't get in with her.' He arched a derisive eyebrow at her expression. 'You have a remarkably sordid imagination. We stopped off at home, and Jenny was practically falling asleep. So I let her catch forty winks in my spare bedroom, while I caught up on some paperwork. In my study,' he added. His eyes showed how much he was relishing her pain. 'Then we had breakfast at the Dorchester, and I brought her here. *C'est tout.*'

Reaction was making Sophie's fingers tremble as she groped for the spoons, and started putting cups out. 'You bastard,' she said in a whisper.

'Poor little Sophie,' Kyle smiled darkly. 'What an innocent you are.' He came over to her, and slid his arms round her in a heart-breaking mockery of tenderness. 'Did you think I was going to make love to her on our first date? That would have spoiled all the fun.'

His touch made her senses swim. 'Do you call this *fun*?' she asked bitterly.

'Of course.'

'I think it's sick. You know I care about you, and you're hurting me in the cruellest way you can think of!'

'*Care?*' he repeated silkily. 'What an interesting choice of words. Are you being extraordinarily naïve, girl? Or are you offering to pay me back in some other way?'

'I don't know what you mean,' Sophie said tiredly.

'Don't you?' He smiled, and touched her chin, tilting her downcast face upward. 'I sometimes could almost believe that you really are a virgin. Now, how could a man find out the truth of that? There's only one reliable way, isn't there?'

'You could just believe me.'

'But I don't believe you.' He was staring at her mouth with intent eyes. 'I don't believe one single syllable that comes out of those soft, sweet, lying lips of yours. I've believed once too often.' He looked into her eyes, and growled softly. 'Why are you looking at me like that?'

'Like what?'

His arms moved to hold her more tightly. 'Damn you, Sophie,' he said softly. 'Those soft grey eyes of yours beg me to make love to you. You know that, don't you?'

'No!' She tried to tear her gaze away, but he held her, as though hypnotised.

'Yes. That would be the only way we could get at the truth of your fabled virginity, wouldn't it?'

'After which,' she said, dry-mouthed, 'the question of virginity becomes irrelevant.'

'It's irrelevant, anyway,' Kyle replied, his gaze hardening. 'You are not the one I'm going to make love to.'

She winced painfully, and caught the flare of satisfaction in his eyes as he saw that his words had struck home.

'But in lieu of that satisfaction,' he said huskily, 'perhaps we could settle for a good-morning kiss?'

She tried to twist her face away from his seeking lips, but he was so strong. His mouth met hers, deliberately erotic as his lips moulded themselves to hers, caressing, pressing warmly and possessively. His hand slid silkily down her back, caressing with calculated sensuality.

'What makes you tremble so much?' he laughed softly. 'The thought of my possessing your delectable little cousin? She's just my type. And she doesn't feel like a marble statue when I kiss her, either. But you'll have to wait, Sophie. I'll tell you when I make love to her, don't worry. But it might not be for a while. Maybe another day or two. Maybe much longer. Who can tell with these things?'

'How can you be so deliberately cruel?' she asked unsteadily, trying to push her way out of his embrace.

'Weren't you cruel to me?' he retorted, his smile tightening. 'Didn't you play exactly this kind of game with me?'

'No, never!'

'Oh, but you did.' His arms tightened, crushing her almost painfully. 'It was a sensational performance. Your professional virgin routine was quite brilliant,' he said, with vitriolic tones in his deep voice. 'You actually fooled me, do you know that? You really are a talented actress, Sophie. For someone like you to convince me that you were a sexual innocent was quite an achievement.'

'It was no achievement.' Sophie's long, dark lashes were wet with unshed tears. 'It was the simple truth.'

'It was a heartless charade.' He kissed her mouth again, but this time cruelly, making her wince as he crushed her lips. 'You had it all at your fingertips—the shy eagerness, the timid touches, the breathy little voice...' He gritted his teeth, as though he wanted to sink them into her throat. 'And then, when you knew that I wanted you, really wanted you, you slipped away, leaving me to read that—that contemptible, insolent little note. Well, I'm going to make you pay for that, Sophie.'

'Perhaps it was contemptible. But what you're doing now is even more contemptible.' A tear slid down her cheek, and Kyle watched it with hard green eyes.

'Tears are a very cheap currency in the theatrical world,' he observed coldly. 'They don't count for much.' His hands slid down to cup her slim waist, drawing her forward. 'However,' he said in a husky rumble, 'they are the first of many, and I must savour my reparation as it comes.'

Sophie's wet lashes fluttered closed as Kyle gathered the tear from her cheek with his lips, tasting the salt of her grief.

The gentle touch of his mouth made yearning flood her aching heart. Her knees buckled, and she sagged against him helplessly, her arms reaching for the hard strength of his man's body.

'Kyle,' she whispered brokenly, 'I need you so much...'

For a taut moment he held her, his mouth pressed against her hair. Then he thrust her away, his eyes glittering.

'It's called frustration,' he said tauntingly. 'Plain, painful, sexual frustration.' It seems we've both got a bad dose of it, my dear Sophie. Except that I have someone who'll relieve it for me. You haven't.' His eyes narrowed. 'Unless you're asking me to do it for you?'

She hated him at that moment. 'I'm not asking you for anything!' The percolator began to bubble, and Sophie turned dully to switch off the gas.

'Isn't that coffee ready yet?' Jenny asked, dancing into the kitchen with a big smile. She looked as fresh and pretty as a daisy, wearing a light cotton dress that made the most of her rather full bust. She nestled up to Kyle with all the possessiveness of a woman confident in her own attractiveness. 'Gosh, I feel better for that shower,' she said, looking up at him.

'You smell delicious,' Kyle said appreciatively, allowing her to mould her lithe body against his. 'I seem to recognise that soap.'

'It's Sophie's.' Jenny lifted her wrist for Kyle to smell her skin. 'Jasmine.'

'It smells different on you,' he smiled, his eyes sultry as they assessed the pretty young girl in his arms.

'I'll bet it does.' Jenny smirked at Sophie. 'Have you been telling Sophie what we did before breakfast?'

'She was intensely curious to know.'

'It was all quite innocent,' Jenny preened. 'But you should *see* Kyle's house, Sophie. It's practically a mansion! Late Elizabethan, you know, all oak panelling and marble floors—and the *biggest* garden I've ever seen in London, going right down to the riverbank.' She turned to look up at Kyle. 'You must be absolutely, impossibly rich, darling!'

'I struggle along. More to the point, where are we going tonight?'

'Somewhere special, darling.' Jenny was obviously delighting in showing off her new intimacy in front of Sophie. 'Somewhere really special!'

'I think I know just the place,' Kyle purred.

'And then,' Jenny giggled, leading Kyle into the sitting-room, 'maybe we can go back to your house again . . .?'

Sophie clenched her mind against the pain. She leaned against the kitchen wall, trying to find a way out. Her instinctive thought was flight. Get out of London, away from Kyle and Jenny.

Yet how could she just leave? She didn't even have her next job lined up, and for the time being she was tied to Joey.

Just how was she going to survive the ordeal that Kyle had planned for her?

CHAPTER SEVEN

'LUCIANI'S offering two and a half per cent of his cut,' Joey Gilmour said, booming down the telephone as usual. 'Since he's entitled to thirty-three per cent net under his contract with the backers, that means you'd be getting less than one per cent of the pre-tax profits. About point eight-three per cent, in fact.'

'That sounds quite respectable,' Sophie suggested.

'Depends what the profit is,' Joey grunted. 'If you'd had point eight-three per cent of his last film, you'd have had point eight-three per cent of blow-all. Look at it this way—*The First Day of Autumn* has to make a hundred thousand profit before you even get eight hundred back. Out of which you have to pay *my* ten per cent. And I don't think all of Luciani's films put together have made that much. We're not talking Hollywood here.' He made a 'tchah' noise. 'Let's not bother with it, Sophie. The man is offering peanuts.'

'I really want to do it, Joey.'

'My advice is to forget it.' Joey had been negotiating with Franco Luciani over the past couple of days, and had rung Sophie at home to give her the benefit of his opinions. 'Listen, the amount of enquiries I'm starting to get about you, you could have your pick of the plums in a month or two. Just sit tight for as long as it takes, and wait for them to drop into your lap.'

'I can't help feeling you're being far too confident about it, and that isn't false modesty. Besides, I want to be working. I can't just sit around here!'

'Listen, this guy is talking about starting filming in mid-September.'

'Yes. He says the light in Tuscany is remarkable at this time of the year...'

'The light in Tuscany?' Joey snorted. 'That isn't why he wants to bring the date of filming forward by six weeks. He's hustling you off to Italy quick-sticks, before you get a better offer. All kinds of people are asking after you, Sophie. It would be far better if you stayed around in London to be on hand for the right opening. If you disappear to Italy to do an art film with Luciani, you might miss something far more important.'

'But this film is important to me.'

'Why?'

'The script is very special. And I've got a feeling about it. I like Franco.'

'Will you do me a favour? Just give me another week to look around before you give Luciani an answer. If I don't come up with anything better, you can think about doing *The First Day of Autumn*. Is that a deal?'

Sophie agreed reluctantly, but as she put the receiver down, she was regretting having let Joey talk her out of an immediate decision. As far as she was concerned, there really wasn't a choice. She needed to take this film.

Even if the script hadn't had a special appeal for her, which it had, she would have jumped at it just to get out of England, and away from her misery. She couldn't face the prospect of sitting around waiting for a better proposal to come along. Not the way she felt right now.

By accepting Franco Luciani's offer, she would be flying to Italy in three weeks' time, and leaving Kyle behind her. Burying herself in work a long way from London was something that appealed very strongly right now.

She glanced at the clock.

'Damn!'

She was due to meet Hélène for lunch in an hour, at the Gay Hussar in Greek Street, a Hungarian restaurant much frequented by journalists, and one of Hélène's favourites. She had a lightning shower in between changing out of her dungarees into a smart dress.

Her own face in the mirror looked tired. There were shadows under the level grey eyes, signs of tension around the full mouth. The past three days had been almost more than she could bear. Pain and anger built up in her to explosion-point sometimes. It was hard to say which was worse—sitting alone in the flat every night while Kyle and Jenny were out, wondering what they were doing; or having to listen while Jenny enthused about last night's entertainments the next day, letting the bitchy side of her nature have full rein as she savoured yet another victory over her cousin.

Right now, thank God, Jenny was still asleep, after dancing till dawn at discos with Kyle.

As far as she knew, they hadn't yet made love. But Kyle was giving Jenny a tour of the most glittering night-spots and the most expensive restaurants, and Sophie knew it couldn't be long before he offered Jenny more. And Jenny, with her casual, open attitude towards sex, would take whatever Kyle offered.

While Sophie watched, helpless.

That Scorpio thirst for revenge: it was so strong. He hardly took his eyes off Sophie when he was at the flat; he was so intent on observing her reactions that he almost ignored Jenny. It was so obvious that his pleasure lay in wounding Sophie, rather than in Jenny's company, that Sophie sometimes wondered how Jenny could fail to notice.

Maybe Jenny *did* notice. She'd always taken intense pleasure in proving herself more attractive to men than her older cousin. Maybe the sense of personal, female triumph made it irrelevant that Kyle didn't really give a damn about her. Maybe it made the pleasure all the more intense. Kyle Hart, after all, was a prize like no other man they'd fought over.

Fought? That was a laugh. There was no competition here. There was no contest at all.

Sophie sighed shakily. Maybe she was being unjust. Maybe Jenny really didn't know how much she was being hurt. But how could she tell her, without spilling out the whole humiliating story of what had happened between herself and Kyle? And how could she trust Jenny not to take even more advantage of the situation, and make her pain all the worse?

She arrived at the Gay Hussar a little late, because the underground trains were running slow, and pushed her way through the crowded entrance. Hélène le Bon was already sitting at a discreet table at the back of the restaurant, but Sophie paused in shock as she registered that Kyle was sitting beside her, laughing quietly over some joke.

A cold wave of reaction gave her goose-flesh, but she forced herself to go on, and even managed a breezy smile as she arrived at the table.

'Sorry I'm late. Have you ordered?'

'Not yet.' Hélène gave Sophie a kiss on the cheek as she sat down. 'Kyle isn't staying for lunch,' she said brightly. 'Too busy making money. But I talked him into stopping for a glass of wine.'

'I'm not crazy about goulash,' Kyle commented. 'And I have clients to see.' His lazy green eyes drifted over Sophie's dress. 'Well, my dear Sophie, you look as fresh as a spring morning.'

'How kind. You look reasonably fit yourself—considering the marvellous time you evidently had last night.'

'"Pleasure and action make the hours seem short,"' Kyle commented calmly.

'*Othello,*' Hélène smiled, 'Act two, scene three. Where did you go last night, Kyle?'

'Dancing with a pretty girl.'

Sophie lifted the menu, her face reddening, and wondered what he and Hélène had been talking about before she'd arrived. Hélène, who had been watching them both with her luminous brown eyes, got to her feet.

'Would you two excuse me a moment? I have a couple of telephone calls to make!'

Kyle's expression was pure irony as he rose and watched Hélène head for the telephones.

'That's called bringing two people discreetly together,' he observed laconically, sitting down again.

Sophie looked at him briefly. He was wearing a dark suit with some kind of old school tie, obviously what he normally wore for work. But the exquisite clothes didn't hide the raw masculinity of the man beneath. In fact, he looked stunning, and that only made her feel all the more tense and ill at ease.

'Is it?' she said coolly.

'Hélène has only one flaw. She thinks that everyone has a right to happiness.'

'And you don't agree?' Sophie said, her long lashes hiding her eyes from him as she scanned the menu.

'I'm a realist. I believe in crime and punishment.'

'I've already gathered that. It's in your stars.'

'The fault, dear Sophie, is not in our stars, but in ourselves.'

'Is it my turn to guess the Shakespearean allusion? *Julius Caesar*, but I don't know the act or scene number.'

'Very good. Hélène thinks that a little honest, civilised talk would iron out all the problems between you and me,' Kyle said drily. He poured her a glass of the dark red wine he'd been drinking. Sophie thanked him, and took a sip. It was strong, almost metallic, but not unpleasant. 'Unfortunately,' he went on, 'she doesn't know that you're not honest, and that I'm not civilised.'

'What nice things you say, Scorpio,' Sophie shot at him angrily.

'My pleasure, Virgo.'

Sophie glanced at Hélène, standing at the telephone with her back studiously to their table, and grimaced. 'Hélène is not going to be back for at least a quarter of an hour,' she said wryly. 'So it looks like we have to talk, if only just to fill in fifteen minutes.'

'Even if the subject matter turns out to be uncivilised and dishonest?'

'I'll risk it,' she replied with a lightness she was very far from feeling. 'You've never even told me what happened with Emma's parents,' she reminded him. 'Have they decided on a divorce?'

'No, poor fools,' he growled. 'They've kissed and made up, and are giving the hoary old myth of happy wedlock another spin.'

'I'm so pleased for Emma's sake,' she said, wincing at his cynicism. 'She must be very happy about it.'

'She's delighted. But then, she's too young to understand the falsity of most human relationships.'

Sophie let that one ride, too. 'Did you go on that cruise with her?'

Kyle picked up his glass and drank briefly. 'After your little disappearing trick, we were both rather dazed,' he said drily. 'It wasn't exactly easy to explain what had happened to an eight-year-old child.'

'Kyle, I'm so sorry——'

'Don't prattle apologies,' he rasped, silencing her. 'As it happened, we left the hotel the same day. Somehow, I just couldn't face staying there another night. Not after you'd——' He bit off what he was going to say. 'We stayed with a friend in Kingston for a few days, then chartered a twenty-eight-foot sloop and spent a week sailing round Haiti. By the time we got back to Kingston, Emma's parents wanted her back, so we flew home to the happy family.'

'Did—did Emma enjoy it?'

'I suppose so,' he shrugged. 'It was a bit of an adventure for her. It did me good, too. Put things back in perspective.'

'Kyle, why can't you believe that I didn't set out to hurt you in Jamaica?' Her voice was low, urgent. 'You think it was some kind of deliberate plan, but it really wasn't like that! It was all so confused. When you didn't recognise me, I—I had this crazy idea to play a joke on you.'

'You consider it a joke,' he said bitingly, 'to go to bed with a man, knowing he thinks you're someone else?'

'I had no idea how we were going to turn out. I thought—I thought you just wanted a holiday romance with me. Something shallow and temporary——'

'That's all I ever did want,' he cut in brusquely. 'Don't kid yourself, Sophie. I never wanted anything more than that from you.'

Silenced, she fought back the tears.

He turned the wine glass absently, watching the scintillating ruby lights on the tablecloth, and went on, indifferent to her unhappiness. 'There was something about you that intrigued me, even in Brighton. You were good company in Jamaica, and you were kind to little Emma. But otherwise...' He shrugged his broad shoulders. 'All I really wanted was a painless affair with a pretty girl. So don't kid yourself that there was ever any chance of anything deeper.'

She fought for self-control in a sea of dizzy nausea. 'Then I'm glad we parted,' she said with an effort, 'before I was discarded for the next pretty face.'

'You haven't been discarded yet,' he said, with a return to that panther smoothness of tone. He smiled into her eyes. 'I haven't finished with you yet. You just watch this space, darling.'

Hélène was heading back to their table, and Kyle rose with an air of finality. 'If I don't leave now,' he said, threat turning to a purr, 'I'm going to offend a very important man in electronic components.' He kissed Hélène's hand, then bent to brush his lips against Sophie's cheek. 'I'm sure we'll see each other again soon,' he said with syrupy politeness, and was pushing his way through the crowds towards the bright street outside.

Hélène met Sophie's eyes guiltily. 'Oh, dear. It seemed a good idea at the time,' she said, covering Sophie's hand with her own. 'Judging by your expression, it wasn't?'

'Not really,' Sophie said, struggling to stitch a smile across lips that were quivering downwards in grief.

'Want to talk about it?'

'Not really.' She got a hanky out of her bag, and stopped any tears before they had time to show. 'Let's just have a lovely lunch, and talk about the theatre, shall we?'

Sophie went in to see Joey Gilmour two days later, and announced that she wanted to do the Luciani film.

He sighed patiently. 'OK, it's a very romantic script, and maybe the finished product will get rave reviews in little arty magazines and student newspapers. But it won't make a penny, I guarantee that. You'll come out with a few hundred pounds in direct fee, and you'll be lucky if you ever get a penny on top of that. I can get you ten times that just doing commercials here in London!'

Sophie was staring at a framed picture on the wall, showing Joey shaking hands with a famous stage actor who had died a year or two ago. 'I've never been to Pisa,' she said absently.

'She's never been to Pisa,' Joey repeated, throwing down his pencil. 'Let me get you a real contract to do a real film. Make a lot of money, then go to Pisa on holiday.'

She smiled at him tiredly. 'I think my mind's made up,' she said, and it sounded almost apologetic. 'I want to do Franco's film. I don't care about the money.'

'OK, so you don't care about the money,' Joey growled, slapping the desk. 'But this is a very important time for you, careerwise——'

'Oh, damn my career!' she said with sudden brittleness.

'I'm not sure I understand you,' Joey sighed, running his hand through his hair. 'You don't look happy lately, Sophie. You're pale, you're withdrawn, you sit there with misty eyes and tell me you don't care about your career—what's up with you?'

'Nothing,' Sophie assured him gently. 'I've just got a feeling about *The First Day of Autumn*. Whether it makes nothing, or makes a million, I know it's the right choice for me.'

Joey stared at her hard, then shrugged. 'OK. I'm not going to argue with you if that's the way you really feel. Do you want me to go ahead with the contract?'

'Yes, please.'

'And you're happy to start in mid-September?'

'Yes. I'll probably only be gone for two months, Joey. Franco wants to get the filming done before the early nights set in, so I'll be back well in time to take up anything else that might come in.'

'It's your life, sweetie. You're going to make one Italian movie director very happy, I can tell you that. The guy has hardly been out of my office this past week. Right, I'll get on to it right away.' He got up to usher Sophie out of his office. 'Just don't do a disappearing trick on me,' he warned, patting her shoulder. 'I'll need a contact number where I can reach you in Pisa, any time of the day or night. Your career is just opening up, kiddo, and you need to stay available.'

On the Tube, she sat thinking about her career, and facing up to the feeling that had been growing in her heart for some time, now. The feeling that she no longer wanted to be an actress.

Oh, yes, she had a certain amount of talent, and once she got established she would presumably always have work. A career lay in front of her, a vocation which might even aspire to success. But she doubted whether she would ever achieve true brilliance. She was no Hélène le Bon. And something had happened to her, something which had given her a deep distaste for her profession.

A life based on illusion, on dreams, a career made out of counterfeiting emotions she did not feel, earning the plaudits of people who did not know her, living lives and saying words that were never her own... Was that what she wanted?

It had all seemed so glamorous to her at eighteen, when she'd signed up for drama school. She'd always had a talent for theatricals, had always aspired to be an actress, but in the five years since then she had changed so much. Especially in the last year; especially since Kyle Hart had entered her life.

Like so many things in life, it wasn't nearly as simple as it had at first seemed. Drama as a pleasant hobby was one thing. Drama as a way of life had to satisfy something deep inside you, or it would only lead to disillusionment and failure. Doing *The Elmtree Road Murders* had been a very mixed experience. Touring with *Here*, *There*, and *Nowhere* had been frankly horrible. Unless you loved the stage, be it theatrical or cinematographic, it was a very hard life. So much depended on illusion, on pretence and imitation. And she was deeply wearied of pretence...

But what else could she do? She wasn't trained for any other kind of work. She couldn't even type or take shorthand. There was no escape from acting, not in the immediate future. She thought about Pisa, and *The First Day of Autumn*. Whatever changes were going on inside her, they would have to wait. The prospect of getting out of London was all that mattered to her right now.

She got off at St John's Wood, and walked slowly back to the flat. It was noon as she rounded the corner of her street, and stopped dead.

Kyle's sleek black Jaguar XJS was parked outside the flat, and Sophie's heart lurched, then sank like a stone into her stomach. Jenny wasn't in; she had gone shopping that morning, and wouldn't be back till later in the afternoon.

Kyle himself was reclining in the driver's seat. His eyes were closed, and Sophie thought for a moment of hope that he was asleep. But as she tried to steal silently past the sports car, his deep voice reached out to her.

'In a hurry?'

'I didn't want to wake you,' she sighed, turning slowly to face him.

'I wasn't sleeping.' Kyle stepped lithely out of the car, more pantherine than ever in a black denim shirt and jeans that moulded the hard, muscled length of his thighs. A thick leather belt circled his taut waist, the heavy brass buckle glinting. He was smiling, the green eyes chips of emerald between thick black lashes.

'Where's your delectable cousin?'

'Shopping,' Sophie said shortly. 'Probably buying smart clothes so you can take her out to smart places, and turn her smart little head.'

'Good. That's what I like to hear.' The smile glinted into a grin, making Sophie's pulses race into turmoil. God, she thought, as she faced him with outward defiance, of all the idiotically emotional women in the world, she must be the most illogical. Why did his mere presence reduce her to trembling shock, when she knew what a bastard he really was? 'Are you going to keep me out here all day?' he enquired, tilting one eyebrow. 'You might offer me a glass of wine.'

In silence, Sophie led him into the flat.

'And what,' he asked, as she busied herself in the kitchen, 'have you been doing all morning, little actress?'

'I went to see my agent,' she said shortly.

'Has he got a job for you?'

'As a matter of fact, yes.' She twisted the cork out of the wine bottle with something like satisfaction. 'I'm going to do the Luciani film.'

His eyes narrowed. 'I heard that the man was hardly offering enough to keep body and soul together.'

She flashed him a dry glance from cool grey eyes. 'You seem to know a lot about my affairs.'

'I hear things,' he said. 'When do you start filming?'

'Next month.' Like him, she was wearing denims, together with a suede jacket over a cotton top. She gave Kyle his glass of red wine, pulled the jacket off, and pushed past him into the sitting-room to hang it on the antique bentwood coat-rack. Kyle watched her movements with unsmiling attention.

'What do you mean, next month?'

'Next month. The month after this one. The middle of September, to be even more precise. I'll be flying to Pisa in a couple of weeks.' She caught the angry glitter that moved like summer lightning behind his eyes. 'What's the matter?' she asked softly. 'Are you annoyed that your prey might be getting away? You've got a fortnight left to torment me in, don't worry.'

'I don't want you escaping too soon.' He came towards her, his expression grim. 'How long will you be gone for?' he demanded roughly.

'Luciani's budgeting on being in Pisa around two months.'

He studied her face with grim attention. 'I'll be waiting for you when you get back,' he said in a threatening growl.

Sophie arched mocking eyebrows, instinctively knowing that she had suddenly gained the upper hand in this vindictive struggle for supremacy. 'Will you? But I may not come back. They say the male lead is quite a man.'

'Luigi Canotta?'

'Hmm.' She folded her arms over her neat breasts and tilted her chin up truculently. 'He's beautiful,' she said lightly. 'I'm looking forward to it very much.'

'Bully for you,' Kyle said, a note of harshness in his voice.

She sensed her advantage, and followed it home. 'Since you know so much about the film, you must know something about the script.' She smiled slightly as he shook his head. 'You don't? Oh, it's a very moving love-story. Very passionate in parts. It opens with me naked in bed with my lover. We've just made love, you see, and he's kissing my breasts... But let me get you the script, and I'll read you the relevant sections.'

She was walking over to get Franco's script when Kyle put his wine glass down and grasped her wrist, swinging her round to face him. 'You little Jezebel,' he rasped, eyes smoking at her like gun muzzles. 'I don't want to see the damned script.'

'Then you'll have to take my word about the passion,' she said, masking her intense triumph with a cool smile. 'Luigi Canotta is exactly the right man to do scenes like that with. Why, I'll hardly have to act at all. I'll just let myself go.'

'You've never let yourself go in your life,' he grated. 'And what would a man like Canotta want with a repressed virgin like you?'

She pulled her hand free. 'I thought I was a Jezebel?' she enquired with maddening poise. 'You're getting your metaphors mixed, Kyle.'

'No, I'm not. Because you're an unlikely mixture of both. Your cousin confirmed the truth for me.' Kyle's eyes gleamed. 'She told me you've never had a man in your life. You *are* a virgin, after all!'

'Well, perhaps that'll change in Italy,' Sophie shot back, her cheeks paling.

'Oh, I see,' he taunted. 'You plan to sacrifice your virginity to Luigi Canotta, on the altar of cinematographic art? Well, Franco Luciani likes the *outré* effects. Perhaps you can persuade him to immortalise the magic moment on film?'

Her free hand flew upwards of its own accord, cracking against his cheek. She'd finally been unable to just take it any more, and the slap must have stung. Kyle caught her wrist swiftly, and pulled her hand to his mouth, twisting it so that he could kiss her open palm.

'That way,' he went on, his eyes as bright as a cat's with amusement, 'we can all share the immortal experience that turns you from a spoilt-rotten little girl into a spoilt-rotten little woman.'

'Stop it!' She tried furiously to slap him again, and almost succeeded. He had to pinion both her hands behind her back to stop her.

'You're quite dangerous,' he said softly, looking down into her face with glinting eyes. 'Do you know something? You may not be as pretty as your sexy cousin, but you're a damned sight more entertaining.'

'Let me go,' she panted.

'In fact,' he drawled, drawing her against his hard body, 'Jenny bores me stiff. But you're something else.'

'Yes! I'm fool enough to be hurt by you, and you enjoy that!' Sophie's eyes flared grey fire at him. 'You accuse *me* of vanity. You've got a nerve, Kyle. Only a man whose vanity was colossal could dream up the sort of sick game you're playing. Why should it matter a damn to me whether you make love to my cousin or not?'

'Why indeed?' he purred. 'Why should I bother with Jenny, when it's *you* I really want to chastise?' He was holding her as close as a lover now, but the muscles of his arms were iron-hard as they immobilised her hands behind her back. 'So you really are a maiden,' he said with a husky laugh, studying her face with dark eyes. 'That changes my outlook about you, my dear Sophie. I now know a far better way of getting back at you.'

'What do you mean?' Sophie demanded angrily.

'You do realise that at your age virginity is tantamount to an aberration?' he asked softly. He was pushing her inexorably backwards as he spoke, forcing her towards her bedroom. 'You're twenty-three, and beautiful enough to make any man desire you. You obviously prize that maidenhead of yours very highly, to have clung to it for so long. What are you planning to trade it for? A wedding-ring?'

'Let me go!' she gasped, struggling vainly against Kyle's superior strength. 'You're hurting me, you brute——'

'But people in glass houses should never throw stones,' he went on, ignoring her protests. 'You obviously don't play poker, my love. Nobody puts their prize asset on the table. Not ever.'

He pushed her into her bedroom, and kicked the door shut behind him, then released her stinging wrists to twist the key in the lock and push it into his pocket.

'Kyle, for God's sake,' she whispered, starting to be really afraid. 'What are you doing?'

'What I ought to have done a long time ago,' he replied. 'What you really want me to do, deep down inside.' He smiled mercilessly. 'I'm going to have that precious prize of yours, my dear Sophie. I'm going to make you a woman.'

'No!'

'I think you mean yes.' His voice was a gentle purr to her sharp denial. 'Don't you want to know what all the fuss is about? Don't you sometimes wonder what it feels like, to be made love to by a man?' He walked over to her, his hands reaching to capture her slim waist. 'A man who knows exactly how to give a woman pleasure in bed?'

'Kyle, you've gone mad!' But she knew those flames that were now beginning to lick in his eyes, and she felt the response shudder through her own body.

'Have I? Then why can I feel you trembling with desire?'

'I'm trembling because you frighten me,' she managed. 'Please let me go, and get out of my bedroom——'

'Not until I've made love to you.'

'You can't force me to submit!'

'I won't have to,' he said with a smoky smile. 'By the time I've finished with you, you're going to be begging me to make love to you. Know that feeling? Like someone burning up with thirst, begging for water. That's the way I'm going to make you feel.'

He bent to kiss her mouth, his lips warm and possessive, the red wine on his breath.

She turned her face wildly away from him, struggling in fierce silence. But it was as though some veil in her mind were being torn open, forcing her to face the truth, that she wanted him, that his mood of raw sexuality was exciting her, sending the hot blood coursing through her veins.

'Do you remember that last time, in Jamaica?'

'I don't want to remember!'

'But I do. I want to remember, because that's where we left off...' Kyle's mouth was roaming across her throat, his lips almost devouring the scented skin. 'That's where we left off,' he growled breathily into her ear, 'and that's where my mind's been stuck for the past month, playing the same track over and over again, driving me crazy!'

She heard stitches rip as he pulled her cotton blouse open with contemptuous power, baring the feminine curves of her bra-less breasts, the dark nipples already thrusting eagerly outwards.

'Kyle, please,' she whispered, feeling sanity start to slip away. 'Don't do this to me!'

'Would you rather I were doing this to your cousin?' He slid his hand into her ruined blouse, and cupped one silky-firm breast in his hungry palm. His thumb slid across the aroused peak, making her whimper with response. 'Would you rather Jenny were in your place right now?'

Sophie pulled the torn corners of her blouse defensively over herself, tormented by his caress. 'No,' she whimpered, her mind reeling.

'Nor would I,' he laughed unsteadily. 'To make love to Jenny would mean nothing to me. But to touch you like this makes me burn inside—just as it makes you burn. Isn't that true?'

'No! You disgust me, you always have done!'

'Is that why you shudder when I touch you here?' He pushed her flimsy defence aside, and had only to caress her breasts to make her body arch with desire against

him. 'Is that why your heart is trembling, like a trapped
bird? Because you feel disgust?'

She tried frantically to fight away from him, but he
merely laughed, deep in his throat, and pushed her back
on to the bed.

'You won't face reality, will you?' With smooth
movements, he stripped off the black denim shirt, revealing the muscled, tanned body that had haunted her
memory for so long. 'You're infatuated with me, Sophie.
You always have been.' Kyle sat beside her on the bed,
his palms smoothing sensuously across the mounds of
her breasts. He smiled down at her, handsome as Lucifer.
'You didn't object the last time I held you in my arms.
In fact, you were melting like ice-cream in the sun. Or
was that all part of the charade, too?'

'No,' she whispered, shrinking from the cruelty of that
reminder. 'It was real.'

'Then why should you find my attentions so un-
welcome now?' he mocked.

'Because in Jamaica you wanted me with passion in
your heart. And now you only want to hurt me!'

Kyle's face darkened. 'Yes,' he said thickly, 'I had
passion in my heart, then. What a fool I must have been,
mooning over you like a love-struck boy. How did you
keep yourself from laughing out loud?'

'I didn't laugh because I felt the same way! Because
it meant something to me, something wonderful!'

'Fabricator.' His voice was like tearing velvet, and
Sophie felt his fingers bite into her arms. He stared down
at the pale oval of her face, his eyes hot green slits. 'You
played your part sublimely well. You're a talented actress. Your only trouble was that you didn't run far
enough, or fast enough, to get away from me.'

'Kyle, *no*,' she begged, as he slowly bent to touch her
breasts with his mouth.

'But then,' he murmured, his breath warm against her
skin, 'you'd have had to run to the other side of the
world to get away from me. And even then, I'd have

come looking for you. How did you ever think you could get away from me?'

The touch of his lips was ruthlessly seductive, making her moan brokenly, her eyes closing.

'I've dreamed of these pale, sweet breasts,' he said raggedly, his lips trailing down the panting valley between them, savouring the taste of her skin. 'The only thing missing is that perfume, that intoxicating smell. Do you know what really hurt me in Jamaica?' He looked up at her, smouldering-eyed. 'You put some of your perfume on that letter. As soon as I opened it, you were there in the room with me. And I couldn't get the smell off my fingers for days...'

'Oh, Kyle,' she said unevenly, 'I'm so sorry.'

'Where is it?' He rose, and stalked over to her dressing-table, long brown fingers searching through the small collection of cosmetics. He found the Giorgio Armani bottle instinctively, and lifted it to his nose. 'Yes,' he said softly, 'this is it.'

He walked back over to where she lay defenceless on the bed. Holding her gaze, he sat beside her again, and took the little glass stopper from the bottle. She flinched as he touched the icy wet tip to her skin, drawing a delicate line of perfume slowly down between her breasts.

The mysteriously seductive smell touched her, flooding her mind with memories. Stronger than wine, it brought the remembrance of that night back into her mind with intoxicating force, reminding her of her own loss, of the paradise she had once lost, and could now have again— at a price.

Kyle smiled, eyes dark as he assessed the effect he'd had on her. He put the bottle down on her bedside table. Then, without further words, he bent to kiss her mouth, hard, crushing her soft lips with ruthless passion. His tongue thrust like a flame between her teeth, plundering the sweet, moist depths of her inner mouth.

Sophie couldn't stop her arms from drawing him close, from clinging to him with trembling passion. She was aching for his possession now, all the pain turning to need.

He was so good to hold, so strong and confident, his maleness filling her senses. She hardly realised that her own nails were biting into the muscles of his shoulders, rough spurs that answered his own igniting need.

She whispered his name, twice, her hands caressing languidly across his warm, naked skin. The third time, his name turned into a gasp that caught in her throat as he caressed the swollen curves of her breasts, then bent to kiss the taut pink tips, anointing them with his tongue, firming them to unbearable hardness in his mouth.

She cradled Kyle's head in her arms, pressing her mouth into the crisp, thick hair, inhaling the clean male scent of him. His hands moulded her hips, drawing her close as he kissed her flanks, the smooth skin of her ribs.

'I've missed you so much,' she whispered. 'I thought I would die without you——' She broke off, arching as his teeth punished her nipples for the tender words.

'No lies,' he rasped. 'Just touch me.' He pulled his belt loose, unfastening the brass button at the waist of his denims. 'Touch me,' he commanded roughly. 'Touch me the way you did before.'

It was if she had no will of her own any longer. Her trembling fingers obeyed, moving timidly down the flat, muscled belly, down the opened front of his denims. The heavy zip slid open, as if eager to admit her.

The delicate touch of her fingers made Kyle arch against her, crying out her name.

'Sophie . . . you drive me crazy.'

It didn't matter that she hardly knew what to do; she had merely to touch her fingertips against the hot, swollen manhood that stretched his briefs to make him shudder with pleasure. Her whole body was trembling now. She hated herself for the way she was responding to him, yet she could no longer stop herself. Kyle was too strong, his effect on her too potent for her to fight.

She lifted her hips unthinkingly as he unfastened her jeans and pulled them down, discarding them on the floor. She was wearing only plain cotton panties with a lace trim, her body tanned and slim against the coverlet.

Groaning her name again, Kyle bent to bury his face against her soft belly, his powerful arms embracing the delicate curve of her hips. He raised himself on his elbow, meeting Sophie's swimming eyes.

'Have you any idea how much I want you?' He caressed her thighs, his palms savouring the silky skin. 'I want you so much that it's a fever.' He lowered his head to kiss the smooth skin of her thighs, close to the lace border of her briefs.

Sophie tried to will her body not to respond, not to betray her, but his touch was so expert, so exquisitely erotic. She shuddered in despair as she felt his tongue trace teasing circles on her skin, his breath warm and quick against her inner thigh.

Shame and grief made a choking sob rise in her throat. Sophie forced it down, covering her eyes with one hand, but she couldn't stop the trembling that shook her whole body.

'What are you trembling for?' Kyle mocked, sliding his thumbs into the lace of her panties, as though he was about to pull them down and expose her nakedness to his kiss. 'Am I hurting you? Haven't you dreamed about me every night since you left Jamaica?'

He must be a sorcerer, to know her mind like that! 'Yes,' she whispered, lowering her hand to look at him with swimming grey eyes. 'But not like this, so cruel and mocking——'

'Sex without love often has both cruelty and mockery in it,' he said brutally. 'Sex is an odd thing, Sophie. A man can dislike a woman, almost hate her...' his teeth grazed her soft skin, making her gasp '...and yet he can also desire her body. In a way, the anger makes the desire all the stronger, all the more potent.'

'It's not a game any more,' Sophie pleaded quietly, knowing this was her last chance to save herself from the destruction of being seduced by a man who hated her. 'Maybe you were justified in thinking I did something really bad to you in Jamaica. Maybe you were even justified in wanting to...to punish me. But you can't justify this, Kyle.'

'Do I have to justify it?' But, as though her unquestionable emotion had touched him in some obscure way, Kyle's hands slowly slid away, releasing her briefs. He moved, freeing her from the weight of his body. Feeling utterly naked and vulnerable, Sophie rolled away from him and curled into a ball of misery, hiding her face in her arms.

'Why are you doing this to me?' she whimpered, desire and pain mingling sickly inside her. 'Have I ever done anything to you that made you feel half as wretched as I feel now?'

'I don't know,' he said in a sombre voice. He watched her in silence for a moment, then went on quietly. 'If I'm wrong about you, then I don't know how you'll ever forgive me. Or how I'll ever forgive myself. But if I'm right about you, then it's no more than you deserve.'

'You're wrong about me,' she said passionately, lifting her head to glare at him with blurred eyes. 'You've been wrong about me from the very start.'

'Have I?' he said with a slow smile.

'You bastard,' she told him shakily. 'I wish to God you'd never come into my life!'

'And that sounds like my cue to leave.' He rose with fluid grace, zipping his denims and clipping the heavy brass buckle of his belt.

'Where—where are you going?' she asked, her chestnut hair tumbled around her face.

'Out of your life,' Kyle said flatly. He reached for his shirt and pulled it on, muscles rippling for an instant before the black denim covered his torso. 'I don't think I need to pursue my vendetta any longer. I've just discovered something—that I can't hurt you without hurting myself. So it's over.'

Her mind tried to grapple with the realisation of what he was saying. She reached numbly for her own jeans. 'What about Jenny, what you said you'd do——?'

'I'm not interested in Jenny,' he said with contempt, tucking his shirt in. 'I never had any intention of taking her to bed. You were all I was interested in. As it turned out, you were too easy to fool. It would only have been fun if you'd shown some spirit.' He turned and watched her as she got into her jeans and pulled a T-shirt out of a drawer.

When she was dressed, Kyle took the key out of his pocket and unlocked Sophie's bedroom door. She followed him out on shaky legs.

'Kyle——'

'What?'

'Will—will I see you again?' she whispered.

'You and I are like oil and flame—a dangerous combination,' he replied. 'We're better apart. We do nothing but harm to each other. I think we've both driven each other a little crazy...'

She hugged her aching breasts, pale-faced. 'Then it's all over?'

'Yes,' he answered indifferently. He walked to the door, and opened it. If he noticed that she was crying, he gave no sign of it. 'Enjoy Pisa,' he said laconically. 'It's a beautiful city.'

'Kyle!'

But he was walking out of her life, just as he had promised. Sophie ran to the door, but he didn't look back. He climbed into the black XJS, switched on the ignition, and drove off down the street without a backward glance.

Sophie was still standing numbly at the doorway of the flat as Jenny came walking up the street from the direction of the tube station. She came up the stairs, lifting her sunglasses into her red-gold hair.

'I've just seen Kyle driving away,' she said suspiciously. 'What the hell is going on, Sophie? What was he doing here?' Jenny looked closer at her cousin. 'You look like a bus just ran over you. Come on, let's get inside.'

Once in the little living-room, Jenny looked around, seeing the bottle of wine, and Sophie's opened bedroom door, the rumpled bed visible inside, the torn blouse on the floor. She stared at Sophie's dazed face, and then grabbed her arm. 'Sophie!' she said in shock. 'Have—have the two of you been making love behind my back?'

Sophie shook her head mutely. Jenny released her arm, her cheeks suddenly pale with anger. 'You're lying! I always knew there was something going on between you and him!' Furiously, Jenny flung herself into the chair. 'I might have *known*!' she snapped. 'I might have bloody well *known*.'

'Jenny——'

'God, I've been such a fool! You were all he ever wanted to talk about. Sophie, Sophie, Sophie. Endless questions about *you*. The man was obsessed with you— and he never so much as wanted to kiss me!'

'We've all gone a little crazy,' Sophie said tiredly, echoing Kyle.

'He was just trying to get at you, wasn't he?' Jenny's blue eyes sparkled with indignation. 'Just wanted to make you jealous enough to get you into bed with him!'

'You don't understand,' Sophie said wearily.

'I understand only too damned well. I've been a patsy.' She glared up at her cousin. 'So you've lost that precious virginity of yours at last. I hope you realise it was thanks to *me*.' She gave Sophie a twisted smile. 'Cat got your tongue? The least you could do is tell me what it was like! Marvellous, I expect.'

'If I told you the truth, you wouldn't believe me,' Sophie said quietly. Tears were flooding her eyes, tears of finality and loss.

'Oh, don't be silly!' Jenny exclaimed. She jumped up and hugged Sophie. 'Losing your virginity isn't such a big deal! You're much better off without the damned thing.'

But Sophie was crying so brokenly that Jenny looked afraid. 'Don't cry like that,' she pleaded. 'I know I've been a bitch to you sometimes, but I really care about you, you know that, don't you?' She hugged her cousin tightly. 'I'm glad you've won for a change. I was starting to think you must be frigid or something.'

Sophie tried to fight back her tearing sobs. 'You don't understand,' she said. 'But it—doesn't matter—any more. It's all over. It's all—over—now.'

CHAPTER EIGHT

THE Leaning Tower of Pisa was something Sophie had seen in countless photographs. It was as familiar to her as Big Ben, or the Eiffel Tower. Yet nothing could have prepared her for the sheer, stunning beauty of the building, with its slender columns of white marble soaring upward, row upon row. Even if subsidence hadn't caused the tower to start leaning sideways, centuries ago, making it an object of wonder, it would still have been one of the great monuments of the world.

As it was, the soft evening sunlight gave the leaning tower a surreal quality, its unlikely profile dominating the other, no less beautiful buildings in the long, grassy quadrangle.

Sophie stared up at it with misty grey eyes as the continuity girl arranged the folds of her skirt. It seemed to her like a symbol of human hope, once tall and lovely, now sinking slowly into absurdity.

She was sitting on the grass, reading Dante, and waiting for her lover.

At least, that was what was written at the top of Scene 217, being shot for the fourth time that evening.

Her lover, at that moment, was sitting a few feet away with a much-stained paper towel round his neck, having his make-up adjusted by Angela, the make-up girl. He was trying to drink a Coke at the same time, and chattering volubly to Franco Luciani over Angela's lean brown arms.

It was hard to keep your romantic illusions about an actor, even one as handsome as Luigi Canotta, once you'd got used to seeing him in a bib stuffed with cotton wool, having greasepaint applied over his features.

Her own face felt slightly stiff under the layer of lightener that made her look so pale. She was now dying. Or meant to be. What would it feel like, she wondered absently, to be really dying, on this romantic evening in early autumn?

It was impossible to imagine. And yet the sadness of Marjorie had entered her soul over the past weeks of filming, making her feel at times infinitely depressed. She had never quite realised just what a tragic script *The First Day of Autumn* was. But then, she hadn't felt quite this sense of acute loneliness when she'd first read it ...

The scene was about to be shot again. The sound crew had checked the little tape recorder concealed in the folds of her skirt, and were now crouching over the bigger machines, headphones on as they listened for any intrusive ambient noise. Angela, the make-up girl, finished with Luigi and picked up her kit, hurrying over to check Sophie's face. A little work with a big, soft brush had the make-up to her satisfaction, and she trotted back to the cameras, calling out. 'They're ready,' to Franco Luciani.

'OK,' Franco said, uncurling his tall frame from the director's chair, 'let's go.'

'Wait!' several people called. The continuity girl pointed upwards. A patch of cloud was moving across the sun, changing the scene.

Everyone waited patiently for the cloud to drift its slow way out of the sky, which was now a clear eggshell blue, fading to yellow near the horizon. A beautiful, Italian sky, Sophie reflected, like skies nowhere else in the world. It was five o'clock in the evening, almost the end of October. She had been in Italy for six weeks, and *The First Day of Autumn* was now nine-tenths in the can. Franco had been true to his word: filming had been swift and without hitches, and within a short while her own part in the film would be over. The crew would be disbanded, and filming would resume in Rome, at the vast complex of studios known as Cinecittá. Sophie herself would soon be going back to England.

As the cloud headed serenely northward, someone started shushing the chattering crowd of tourists who were watching from behind the rope barrier that had been erected around the set.

Something like silence gradually prevailed. Sophie caught Luigi Canotta's eye, and he grinned at her. Over the past six weeks they had struck up an excellent rapport. Apart from a general conviction that he was God's gift to women, he was a likeable, amusing boy. Only three or four years older than Sophie herself, he was also a talented actor with whom she'd enjoyed working.

'OK,' Franco called, finally satisfied that all was well. 'Ready, Sophie?'

She nodded. Everyone was speaking Italian, but she'd learned enough in the past month and a half to understand everything that was said to her. Or almost. There had been a few mix-ups, but luckily these had been comical rather than disastrous.

One of the sound men lowered a foam-wrapped microphone on a long boom until it was hovering over Sophie.

'Cameras...action!'

She was staring at the book as the scene began, reading the beautiful lines of poetry. There wasn't much dialogue in this scene, but the action had to be convincing. These were the scenes she hated most, the scenes in which she had to counterfeit physical passion. Sometimes it was only with an effort that she could get through them, and Luigi's easygoing sense of humour really helped.

Luigi Canotta walked across the grass towards her. As his shadow touched her she looked up, smiled, and held out her arms to him.

Laughing, he sat down beside her and embraced her. They kissed, mouths miming passion as Sophie slowly sank down on to her back, Luigi on top of her.

As had always happened, at moments like this Sophie's mind flooded with thoughts of Kyle. With memories of *his* kisses, *his* touch. The rush of emotion was intense, covering her skin with goose-flesh. She had to force her mind to forget Kyle, and to relinquish the shuddering remembrance of how it had been with him. This was here, now. This was fiction.

One of the cameras had dollied forward on its tracks, and was now zooming slowly in for a close-up over Luigi's shoulder. The kiss broke off.

'What are you reading?' Luigi asked. The script was all in English; an Italian version would later be dubbed for distribution on the Italian circuits.

'Dante,' she told him, looking up at him with adoring eyes.

'Dante?' he laughed. 'Why does an English girl read Dante?'

'Because he speaks of our love,' she replied. Had she really once thought this corny script so touching? Or was she just getting blasé about it?

They clinched again, lips meeting in kisses that grew longer and more passionate. Sophie's arms twined themselves around the young Italian's neck, her eyes closed as she feigned the abandon of a woman in love.

But she was not a woman in love. In the cinema, months away, it would seem like a highly emotional scene. But to Sophie, right now, it meant almost nothing. She was thinking how absurd kisses were when there was no emotion to give them a meaning: grinding contacts of lips and teeth, empty and uncomfortable.

The kiss went on for longer than in the first three takes. Franco must be pleased with the way this take was turning out. Imprisoned by Luigi's embrace, Sophie was growing self-consciously aware of his body on top of her own. She could hear his breathing, taste the sweet trace of Coca-Cola on his mouth. She waited tensely for the end of the take, her hands restlessly caressing Luigi's back.

At last, Franco's voice broke into the silence.

'Cut!' he called, and came over as Sophie and Luigi broke their clinch. She had to restrain herself from wiping her mouth in distaste. She didn't want to hurt Luigi's feelings.

The director was smiling broadly. 'Excellent,' he nodded. 'Just right. We'll stop there for tonight—the light's going. I'll check the rushes tomorrow, but I think that last take is going to be just perfect.'

Luigi was pulling grass out of his clothing. He grinned. 'Pity. I was just getting into that scene.'

Sophie smiled, getting to her feet. It was Luigi's usual joke. In fact, they had already played far more intimate scenes, in bed. Luigi had been completely naked for some of them, Sophie herself wearing only briefs. She just hadn't had the depth of professionalism to carry off those scenes without embarrassment. Somehow, pretending to make love to a strange man in front of a watchful crew of ten or fifteen technicians had always made her feel acutely uncomfortable. She suspected it always would. Just what kind of actress, she wondered, was she?

'Tomorrow afternoon,' Franco was saying to Sophie, 'we'll start working on the hospital scenes. I'd like to have a short script conference tomorrow morning, to discuss some aspects of your part. OK, Sophie?'

'Fine,' she nodded.

'I'll run you home as soon as you are ready. Be waiting for you in the car.'

'Thanks, Franco,' she smiled. She borrowed cleanser from Angela, sat down on one of the canvas chairs, and started taking off her make-up amid the general confusion of packing up.

The heavy canisters of film were being unloaded from the cameras, and the road crew had moved into action, dismantling the other equipment for the evening.

They were moving location tomorrow. With the illogicality of film-time, the sequel to scene 217 had already been shot, a few days ago. They'd come to the Leaning

Tower this evening because, it being a Wednesday afternoon, there would be the fewest tourists.

When she was ready, she gathered her belongings into her kitbag, said goodnight to Luigi and the crew, and walked over to Franco's big silver Mercedes-Benz. As he drove her through the busy centre of Pisa towards her hotel, which was out in the countryside, Franco was eagerly discussing the next phase of filming. The hospital scenes were the last in the film; Marjorie was to overdose on heroin and be rushed into a clinic, where she was destined to die.

The 'clinic' was actually a beautiful sixteenth-century *palazzo*, now an old-age home run by nuns, in which Franco had hired a floor for a week. He was very enthusiastic about the setting, which was admittedly beautiful.

But then, old buildings in this part of Italy had so much charm. Even her hotel was exquisite; it never failed to lift her heart to come back to the Pensione D'Este after a tiring day's filming. An old Tuscan farmhouse set among cypresses, it had immense charm.

She said goodnight to Franco and went up to her room, which overlooked a central courtyard. Just at the level of her windows a huge pergola supported a leafy vine, which was now heavy with dark grapes. If she'd wanted, she could have reached out and plucked one of the dusky fruits...

She showered, and got into a loose cotton dress, then went downstairs to the dining-room. There were no more than half a dozen guests, and it was a quiet evening. She ate a light supper of minestrone followed by fresh strawberries. Her appetite was practically non-existent these days, which was all to the good. The extra-slender pallor made her performance as Marjorie all the more convincing...

A week. Not much more than that, and she would be going back to England. Back to everything she had left behind her.

She didn't want to go home. Her memories were still acutely painful.

The weekend after that last scene with Kyle was still rather hazy in her mind. Jenny and she had hardly spoken. Still put out at having 'lost' Kyle to her cousin, Jenny had been offended that Sophie was unwilling to discuss what had happened. It was so natural for Jenny to boast about her conquests of men that she hadn't been able to comprehend that Sophie wanted to keep her experiences with Kyle private.

Eventually, they'd made it up, but by then Jenny's feelings had been hardly relevant any more. Sophie's sense of hurt and loss had been impossible to shed. More than ever, she had been overwhelmed by her sorrow, her incomprehension, and her hopeless love for Kyle.

It was now almost a whole year since they'd first met, in Brighton, and Sophie realised that for those twelve months he had hardly been out of her thoughts for a single day. He had haunted her from the first moment they'd met. In that long spell between Brighton and Jamaica, she had dreamed of him, and for three miraculous weeks in Jamaica he had been hers.

Even the savage period of his 'game' with Jenny had made her love him still further. She would rather have Kyle tormenting her than not have him at all. Than have this emptiness, this vacuum ...

How had it all turned so sour? When she looked back at the decisions she had taken, at the way she had left him, with that cool little note, she found it almost impossible to explain her own behaviour. She'd treated it all like a game, but it hadn't ever been a game. Kyle's feelings for her had been deep and true, and she'd made a mockery of them.

The truly sad thing was that she knew in her heart that Kyle's feelings towards her were still profound. He would never have expended so much passion on trying to wound her if he hadn't really still cared, deep down. That Scorpio temper ... what a tragic waste.

He was out of her life now, forever. She lived in dread that one day she would hear, or read, of his marriage. That was a blow that she truly dreaded. How could she not dread it? Kyle was the only man she had ever loved, and she would never stop loving him, not until the end of her days.

She tried not to think about Kyle at all, but the memories were obtrusive, and she had been in the habit of dreaming about him for so long that it was almost impossible to break. His loss made her whole future seem so dark, so without hope. What *was* her future? Where did the path forward lie? Sometimes she felt she could not see it at all...

These past weeks in Tuscany, she had been feeling more and more insecure as an actress. She had lost something vital, the will to impersonate someone else's feelings, and it astonished her sometimes that Franco and the others couldn't detect that. At times she felt utterly naked, the script empty words in her mouth, her actions mechanical and without life.

What was she going to do when she got back to London? Joey kept promising great things, but she felt so unprepared for any more work that she didn't know what she was going to say to him. Maybe she would go home.

It was months since she'd been with her parents. Maybe a few weeks in Scarborough, listening to that gravelly North Sea rhythm, would help clear her cloudy head. She was beginning to see why nervous breakdowns were so common in the acting profession. Once you began to doubt yourself, the strain on you became enormous...

She went up to her room after dinner, and stared at the pages of a book. As the Italian dusk deepened, the sweet trill of a nightingale sounded from the distant cypresses, to be answered by another, then another...

Enchanted by the exquisite song, she put down her unread book, and went to the window.

The evening sky was deep violet, streaked with gold and crimson. A soft, warm breeze was blowing, smelling of the distant Mediterranean.

While the twilight gathered, a deep peace stole all around. As she looked down into the courtyard, her heart faltered.

A tall figure was standing under the pergola, looking up at her window. A figure so like Kyle that she thought she must be dreaming. She laid a hand instinctively over her suddenly racing heart.

'Kyle?' Eyes wide with shock, she stared for a few seconds longer, then turned and ran to the stairs. She was praying that it wasn't a mirage as she raced down the tiled staircase, her breath fast and uneven. Would he be there when she got down? Had he been a figment of her grieving heart's imagination?

She pushed the door open, and stepped out into the twilit courtyard, her mind spinning. It hadn't been an illusion.

Kyle was standing where she had last seen him, motionless, a dark, tall figure that had haunted her mind for so long. They stared at each other tautly for a long moment. She couldn't speak for emotion.

Then he walked slowly over to her, those deep, beautiful eyes staring down into her face. 'God help me,' he said huskily. 'You're so very beautiful, Sophie.'

'Kyle, what——?' Her voice caught in her dry throat. 'What are you doing in Italy?'

'Looking for my salvation.' He looked tired, and his chin was dark with stubble. The jacket he was wearing was grey vicuña, soft as a cloud. He reached out to touch her face with gentle, almost hesitant fingers. 'Looking for forgiveness from a woman whom I've hurt beyond forgiving. Looking for you, Sophie.'

'Oh, darling,' she whimpered, melting into his arms, almost too stunned to take his presence in.

His arms wrapped around her, the way they'd done in countless dreams. Except that this was real.

'Can you forgive me for my stupidity and cruelty?' he asked huskily, his mouth pressed into the fragrant curls of her hair. 'Since you left, I've ached for you until I thought I'd go out of my mind...'

'There's nothing to forgive,' she whispered.

'I've been standing out here, trying to gather the courage to come in and see you.' His voice was strained. 'I—I didn't know how you'd receive me.'

Curious faces were peering at them from the windows. 'Come up to my room,' she begged shakily. 'We can't talk here!'

She took his hand, and led him up to her little room, now bathed in the crimson and gold of the sunset. As she shut the door behind them, Kyle took her in his arms with the urgency of a drowning man, and started covering her face with kisses. Sophie clung to him, gasping at the male passion she felt in the rigid muscles of his body.

'I love you,' he whispered, his mouth finding hers for a dizzyingly deep kiss. 'I've lain in bed dreaming of you beside me, and waking to loneliness and regret. I told myself to wait until you got back from Italy, but I couldn't stay away. I had to come and find you. I've been in Italy for two days.'

Her eyes were closed in bliss. She felt as though a pain of months had suddenly been taken away, to be replaced by a throbbing delight. 'Why didn't you come to me as soon as you got here?'

'I had to pluck up the courage.'

'Do you need courage to face me?'

'I need courage to face how much I need you, how much I adore you... I stood among the crowd watching you working yesterday and today. Watching that boy pretend to be your lover——' His arms tightened, their formidable strength almost crushing her. 'It tore me apart. I thought I'd die, standing there, seeing another man kissing you, holding you in his arms, making love to you——'

'Oh, Kyle! None of that is real!'

He cupped her face in his hands, kissing her mouth. 'I've thought so many times of that threat you made—that you'd have a love-affair with Luigi Canotta——'

'Of course I haven't done that,' she laughed unsteadily. 'It's all only fiction, my love,' she said, looking up at him with eyes that were filling with tears of unbearable emotion.

'With you, I can no longer distinguish between what is real and what is fiction,' he said quietly. 'All I know is that without you my life is a barren wilderness, without hope. I can't go on without you, Sophie. I love you, with all my heart and being. I want us to put the dark past behind us, and enter the future together.' He drew a deep, ragged breath. 'I want you to marry me.'

Joy filled her, making her legs weak. If this was a dream, and she woke up alone, she would kill herself.

'I'm yours, Kyle. I always have been! Oh, Kyle—you don't have to marry me. Just let me be close to you!'

'Close?' He touched her wet eyelashes with his lips. 'My love, I'm going to grapple you to my soul with hoops of steel. For God's sake, tell me you forgive me for the way I behaved in London!'

'I forgave you even before you hurt me,' she said softly.

'How much I must have made you suffer. I was half mad, my darling. During that bloody awful cruise with Emma, I just brooded and burned. I got no sleep, no peace. I swore I'd have a terrible revenge on you for doing that to me. When I got back to London, I wanted to come round to your flat and tell you exactly what I thought of you. But I didn't trust myself not to weaken and break down. I had this horrible vision of me making a fool of myself in front of you, telling you how much I loved you—and you laughing in my face!'

'How could you ever have had such an idea about me?' she asked numbly.

'My mind was distorted with pain and disappointment. It was that Scorpio need to strike back that you once spoke about. All I could think of was punishing you, even though somewhere, deep down beneath my anger and hurt, I knew that you really did care about me. When Hélène mentioned your cousin Jenny, I suddenly realised how I could get at you.'

Sophie shuddered. 'You chose a very cruel weapon. When I thought I'd lost you to Jenny, my heart almost broke.'

'God forgive me,' he whispered. 'As if I could ever have any serious feelings towards that feather-brained little flirt...' He drew her close, his lips closing on hers. 'I adore you. I can't live without you.'

'I'm the one who needs forgiveness,' Sophie whispered, a long while later. 'What I did in Jamaica was imbecilic. But I was so afraid, Kyle. So afraid of losing you that I had to run away. I didn't know how deep your feelings were. I didn't think they could possibly be as deep as mine!'

'Sophie...' They sank down on to the bed together, Kyle's magnificent face tight with emotion. 'That night in Ocho Rios, the night before you left...I was going to ask you to marry me.'

She felt the blood drain from her heart. 'Kyle!'

'I'd only known you three weeks—or so I thought. But I knew there would never be anyone like you again. I started to get terrified of losing you. I had this sort of nightmare that one day you would suddenly be gone.' He pulled a wry face. 'Little did I know how soon that nightmare was going to come true! I wanted to ask you to be my wife after we'd made love. But things didn't work out that way. I told myself I would ask you the next day. I spent hours lying awake, and rehearsing a stupid little speech. And I, too, was terribly afraid. I knew you wanted me, but it was so hard to tell how deeply you cared. If at all. You were so mysterious, so hard to fathom. You made me feel so uncertain, so clumsy——'

'My love,' she said brokenly, 'I had no idea. Oh, if I'd only known!'

'After you left, it was as though my soul had been poisoned,' he went on, shaking his dark head. 'I was so bitter, so desolate. I wanted to come racing after you, but my pride wouldn't let me. It took a long while for it to sink in. Sophie Aspen, not Sophie Webb. The Sophie I fell in love with in Jamaica was the same girl I'd once laughed at in Brighton.' His eyes were dark as they looked into hers. 'Well, I've paid for my folly, my darling. If I hurt you in Brighton, if I was stupid and blind and didn't look beyond appearances, you made me pay tenfold in Jamaica. I've never felt so crushed in my life.'

'I was afraid that once you knew who I really was you'd lose interest in me,' she said in a husky voice. 'I thought it might happen all over again—that you'd find me absurd and ridiculous——'

'Sophie.' He took her hands. 'When I met you in Brighton, you were an overweight girl in heavy spectacles, wearing shabby clothes, with lank black hair. You were a strange creature, then. So drab and plain. Even when you came off set, Maisie still seemed to hang over you. You were uncertain and shy, yet there was something about you that intrigued me. What I saw on that beach in Ocho Rios was an exciting, beautiful woman with a slender body and chestnut hair. Tanned, poised, graceful, hiding mysteriously behind dark glasses. It was nine months later, in another world. Do you find it so hard to understand how I didn't recognise you?'

'I was still the same person,' she smiled tremulously.

'Yes.' His expression was bitter. 'I've been so blind. When I first met you in Brighton, I should have seen beyond appearances. I should have listened to the voice in my heart that was telling me you were something special, something wonderful. But I let you slip through my fingers. I hurt you then, and I hurt you in London—but I swear I'll never hurt you again.' He paused, gathering his thoughts. 'Remember that I told you I hadn't watched *The Elmtree Road Murders*? Well, of course I did watch it. There was no ladyfriend. And while I watched, I had the weirdest feelings. I was remembering it all so clearly. Remembering you, in Brighton. There was something so familiar about you, when we next met in Jamaica. I was sure I knew you well, but I could never put my finger on it. You appearance had changed so much that it was impossible for me to recognise you as Sophie Aspen. And the longer I was with you, the harder it got for me to pin-point that mystery. I thought that this feeling that I knew you was natural, because we were so perfectly suited. I didn't realise that I was already in love with you.' His voice gentled. 'But I didn't fall in love with your face or your figure. I fell in love with *you*, with the woman you are inside. And I've realised something else over these past few weeks of misery—that if I'd only got to know you better in Brighton, I would have fallen in love with you then.'

She laughed quietly. 'The idea of magnificent, passionate Kyle Hart falling in love with ugly little Maisie Wilkin is crazy!'

'Not so crazy. You were in disguise, though. You fooled me, not once, but twice! Sophie, my sin lay in not looking beyond appearances. My only plea is that it's a very common male fault. We men are fools. We tend to judge women through our eyes, rather than through our reason. We're terrible blockheads that way. All I can say is that your appearance made it easy for me to get to know you in Jamaica. And to know you was to love you. I've learned my lesson. You're the only woman I have ever wanted to marry. The only woman who ever got through my defences far enough to make me feel an emotion I thought I could never feel, an emotion that I thought was beyond me...love.' He brushed his lips over her half-open mouth. 'I've never

known love before. I never will again.' Their kiss
deepened. She felt his hand cup her breast, caressing the
soft curve with trembling hunger. 'I'm madly, irrevo-
cably in love with you, Sophie,' he whispered. 'I want
to spend the rest of my life proving it to you. And I'm
not leaving here until you say you'll marry me.'

'You're not leaving me at all, not ever. Not ever again.
And yes, I'll marry you, my love. Without you I'm
nothing, you see. If I don't marry you, I'll just wither
up and die, and blow away on the wind...'

She clung to him, arching her neck ecstatically as he
kissed the hollow of her throat, that favourite place he
so loved to kiss. She ran her fingers through the thick,
crisp roots of his hair, just losing herself in the scent
and the feel of him. Suddenly, they didn't need any more
words. Clinging together, they sank back on to the bed,
mouths seeking, kissing, adoring. The tension of long
separation was starting to coil like a spring between them,
making them ache for release.

'We'll marry as soon as we get back to London,' he
was planning thoughtfully. 'How much longer must you
stay here?'

'A week.'

'Just enough time to get a really big wedding on the
go! But...does that boy have to kiss you again?' Kyle
asked, dark eyes searching hers.

She smiled dreamily. 'Luigi? Hardly. There's only a
week's filming left, and Marjorie has to die soon. Quite
appropriate, really, when you think that Sophie is starting
a new life.'

The emeralds of his eyes were bright with love and
amusement. 'My little actress, how I love you!'

'I'm only an actress for one more week.' She was
deadly serious as she looked into his eyes. 'I want nothing
more than to be your wife, Kyle. I don't have any am-
bitions after that. This is the last film I'll ever make,
Kyle. I'm never going to act again. From now on, I only
want reality—the reality of our love.'

'Sophie, that isn't what I want,' he said gently, caressing her slim flanks.

'It's what I want,' she replied tenderly. 'I just can't do it any more. I was getting desperate. I don't want anything except truth from now on. I don't want anything that will take me away from you, not for so much as a day. I don't ever want to have to kiss another man, or to have to pretend another love. I'm going to take marriage to you very seriously, Kyle. I'm going to put every ounce of myself into it. Into loving you, loving our children, making sure nothing ever goes wrong again——'

'Nothing ever will,' Kyle vowed.

'Make love to me,' she whispered.

His eyes glittered. 'Here? Now?'

'Here and now. I've waited so long that if I have to wait any longer I'll go mad!'

He was kissing her throat, his fingers flicking open the buttons of her dress. 'Don't you want to be a virgin on your wedding-day?' he whispered.

'No,' she said simply, 'I want you, now!'

'Scorpios have stings, little virgin.'

'Go on,' she invited, her eyes dreamy as he started kissing her naked breasts. 'Sting me . . .'

The twilight had deepened into velvety darkness. In the deep blue sky, a golden moon slowly rose over the Italian cypresses until it was high enough to shine in at an open bedroom window, where two lovers were learning the old, secret, mysterious language of love. But the moon was too old to be shocked by anything it saw through open bedroom windows . . . and the lovers never even noticed.

HARLEQUIN
Romance®

Coming Next Month

#3097 SOCIETY PAGE Ruth Jean Dale
The last person Annie Page wants to work for is newspaper publisher Nick Kimball, her late husband's sworn enemy. Still, any job is better than none when you're broke. What she doesn't foresee is enjoying the job—or falling in love with Nick.

#3098 LOVE THY NEIGHBOUR Victoria Gordon
Their first meeting was explosive, and Fiona Boyd resolves to avoid millionaire sheep farmer Dare Fraser as much as possible. Realizing her dream of independence proves difficult, however, since Dare turns out to be the man next door.

#3099 A SECOND LOVING Claudia Jameson
Happily engaged to Alan, Emma never questions the strength of her feelings for him until she arrives in America to nurse her convalescent brother. When she meets her brother's blond Viking of a neighbor, Tor Pedersen, there is no need for words....

#3100 BURNING DREAMS Peggy Nicholson
When Kara Tate's father manages to burn down a Stonehall stud barn, Texas pride leaves Jordan Stonehall satisfied that his father's old enemy will rot in jail. But Kara has a plan for restitution—one a man like Jordan Stonehall is honor bound to accept....

#3101 A WOMAN'S PLACE Nicola West
TV producer Marc Tyrell makes it clear that he expects Jan to swallow her principles and acknowledge that he's the boss. But Jan figures men have had their own way for too long—and she has other ideas!

#3102 BOND OF DESTINY Patricia Wilson
Victoria's teenage dreams of marrying Damien Hunt shattered when she discovered that he and her grandfather had planned the marriage for the sake of their family business. She ran away to a new life, but six years later, when Damien finds her again, she can't help but wonder what his motives are this time.

Available in January wherever paperback books are sold, or through Harlequin Reader Service:

In the U.S.
901 Fuhrmann Blvd.
P.O. Box 1397
Buffalo, N.Y. 14240-1397

In Canada
P.O. Box 603
Fort Erie, Ontario
L2A 5X3